BOOKS BY ADRIENNE RICHARD

Pistol
The Accomplice
Wings
Into the Road

Into the Road

))) Into))) the Road

by
ADRIENNE RICHARD

An Atlantic Monthly Press Book
Little, Brown and Company
Boston   Toronto

LIBRARY OF CONGRESS CATALOG CARD NO.

FIRST EDITION

T 10/76

Excerpt from *Bike Fever* by Lee Gutkind. Copyright © 1973 by Lee Gutkind. Used by permission of Follett Publishing Company.

Library of Congress Cataloging in Publication Data

Richard, Adrienne.
Into the road.

"An Atlantic Monthly Press book."
SUMMARY: When his brother returns home on a motorcycle after six years, Nat decides to buy one too and spend the summer traveling with him.
[1. Motorcycling—Fiction] I. Title.
PZ7.R378In   [Fic]   76-25911
ISBN 0-316-74318-6

ATLANTIC–LITTLE, BROWN BOOKS
ARE PUBLISHED BY
LITTLE, BROWN AND COMPANY
IN ASSOCIATION WITH
THE ATLANTIC MONTHLY PRESS

*Published simultaneously in Canada
by Little, Brown & Company (Canada) Limited*

PRINTED IN THE UNITED STATES OF AMERICA

This book is for my son Daniel (BMW)
and my son Ran (BMW),
who turned me on to bikes
and tuned me in to the road.

Contents

Part One
BREAKING IN
(or Out or Maybe Even Open)

Part Two
GETTING INTO IT

Part Three
BRINGING IT TOGETHER

 Part One

BREAKING IN
(or Out or Maybe
Even Open)

❦ 1 ❧
One
Direction

Around here it ain't easy.

— Uncle Joe

Nathaniel Coombs loped up the subway steps, and as he neared the top, he took his hands from the pockets of his letter jacket and became aware of what he saw from the corners of his eyes. He did this without slowing down, without thinking, as he burst into the late spring sunlight of Orient Square. He had learned a long time ago how to avoid being jumped. Even the broad daylight and afternoon traffic of the square did not prevent his instinctive preparation.

Dodging between a van and a car, he cut across the street from the island where the subway exits opened their dark jaws. From the doorway of Samuels's furniture store the owner studied him suspiciously. "You going to graduate, Nat?" he asked.

"Two weeks to go," Nat said, and grinned cheerfully, thinking, What's that look supposed to mean? I never took anything. But he had thought of it, and Mr. Samuels knew — he suspected. Nat didn't stop.

Two kids sitting on the tailgate of a delivery truck watched him coming along the sidewalk.

"Here he is," one of them called out, and the other yodeled, "Our hero!"

Nat picked up a stone and pretended to take aim. When his arm came through, somehow the rock slipped from his fingers and skinned the side of the truck. He hadn't meant to do that. "Good eye!" they jeered, but a note of admiration and envy sounded, too.

What's the matter with me, Nat thought, turning the corner. Was something inside about to break open? His body tensed against it. Ahead he saw the familiar red-on-white plastic sign that proclaimed

GIUSEPPE'S DELI

and he thought, if I can just make it before it happens. He had thought that times without number in the past. He had always made it and he did now, but this time what he was afraid of went with him through the door.

A little string of bells jingled. His uncle Giuseppe leaning against the chopping block behind the counter looked up at the sound. Before him a policeman sat over coffee and cannoli.

His uncle's face warmed. "You're home early. I thought you stay at school late today. I thought you sign yearbooks till your hand falls off."

"There's a big signing party tonight at the Knights of Columbus. I guess I'll go to that." He spoke to Officer Flanagan as he passed into the little room at the back.

His uncle called out, "You got a postcard."

At that moment Nat saw it stuck behind the hook where his apron hung. He stood for a few minutes looking at it, not taking it in his hand. He knew who had sent it. In six years he had never received anything but postcards from his brother, Cyrus. They gave him a curious feeling, as if his brother were a radio in space sending a weak intermittent signal, one that activated something strange inside him.

His own turbulence affected his picture of Cyrus. He had no clear notion of what he looked like. His last precise memory was of Cyrus leaning across the counter where Officer Flanagan sat now and taking Uncle Joe by his apron and saying, "I stay till I get through. Then I split." Nat remembered the ice in his tone better than the words he spoke.

He had watched Uncle Joe's dark face darken further, and for a moment he was terrified that he might reach behind him for a knife. Uncle Joe had shoved Cyrus back and cursed him in two languages, but he didn't strike him. For a month Cyrus had stayed around. Then he had vanished, leaving Nat behind.

Looking at the line of snowy peaks on the postcard, Nat felt the old resentment against his brother. He turned the card over. "The Grand Tetons Seen from Moose, Wyoming" was printed on it. Beneath it was scrawled

See ya soon

Cyrus

He studied the message, wondering how far Moose, Wyoming, was from Boston, feeling again the fright and loss of six years ago. Cyrus had been his protector, had saved him from getting beaten up, roughed up, robbed, chased. Then suddenly he was gone, and Nat faced the asphalt playgrounds and dark sidewalks alone. Well, he learned. By keeping a couple of dimes, a quarter sometimes, in his pocket he bought his own protection. By running like hell toward that red-on-white deli sign. Then one September he discovered he was a head taller than everybody else, a little heavier, better at sports. After that they left him alone, but his reflexes never unlearned their protective behavior.

"See ya soon," Cyrus had written. Nat wasn't sure he wanted to see him, ever. Still, he ached to know where Cyrus had been for six years, to unravel the mystery that was his brother. Hanging his jacket on the hook, he heard Officer Flanagan say, "You're lucky with that one, Joe. That's a good kid."

"Better than that," his uncle said.

"It does you good to see a kid pointed in the right direction. A kid like Nat makes my work easier. Proves you can go straight around here."

"It's Rose that done it. She taught him to speak good."

"My kid brother, Richard, he just joined the force in Lowell."

"You set a good example. Around here it ain't easy."

"Where's that brother of Nat's? You ever hear from him?"

"Not for six years — we hear nothing."

Nat slipped the apron over his head and tied the strings, feeling along with the old resentment against Cyrus and the old disgust with himself for getting left, a new anxiety and attraction and inferiority. After all, what had he, Nat, been doing for six years? Going to school, sports, working in the deli, avoiding trouble, the straight life. He moved behind the counter.

The bells jingled, the door slammed, and someone said, "Two hot special combos with plenty of Russian."

"Stay or go?" Nat asked, pulling the parts of himself together again. He felt a little surprise that the customer knew the answer.

"No! No! Today you don't have to help!" his uncle cried. "Go around and sit down. I make the subs."

"You make one, and I'll make the other," Nat said, smiling.

"Okay! That's the way we always do it. We do it today, too."

Reaching into his pocket for his change, Officer Flanagan asked, "Who makes the best, you or your uncle?"

"He does," they answered in one voice, and everyone broke into laughter.

"He showed me about the Russian dressing," Giuseppe said. "I know nothing about this Russian, but everybody likes it. It's good for business."

Nat laughed, slicing green pepper with a big knife. He liked to work side by side with his uncle, both of them doing the same things, slicing, chopping, loading the oval buns with sausage and pastrami. When they were ready, he slid the two subs into the oven to heat and afterward wrapped them in white paper. You could smell the garlic and spices and warm bread through it. Then he rang the cash register with the sale. Working the register was the first thing Uncle Joe had let him do in the delicatessen, punching the keys with the numbers, hitting the total key and listening to the inner works ringing, and watching the little flags with the amount of the sale pop up on top, always leaving the bills on the little shelf while he made the change, counting it into the customer's palm. "When they eat, we eat," Uncle Joe had said. Nat still felt a satisfaction as the register rang under his fingers.

The afternoon crowd had thinned and the supper buyers

hadn't come in yet when Aunt Rose backed through the door, her arms around packages. They stood back and smiled at her as she dropped her bags on the counter, sat down with an "ooof" on a stool, and put her head in her hands. "What a day! I am beat."

Uncle Joe poured her some coffee with milk while Nat took the lid off the Italian cookies, choosing one for himself as he put them on the counter. Aunt Rose straightened up and looked at him.

"You have a good day, Nat?"

"Pretty good."

"How about here?"

"Plenty business."

She sipped her coffee. "Anything more from Cyrus?"

Nat laid the postcard on the counter beside her cup. "He was in Moose, Wyoming."

"There's no such place," said Uncle Joe, and Nat felt that his uncle wished there was no such Cyrus, either.

Smoothing her poofed black hair, his aunt read the card, studied the picture and set it down again. "He's your brother, he's my sister's own boy, and he'll be different from when we saw him last. Six years is a long time. He's a man now. We just have to make a place for him. He won't stay long, but it'll be good for us to see him. After all he's your brother, Nat. A brother's a brother."

His uncle leaned against the chopping counter with his arms folded and his dark eyes on Rose. "Rose is right. We steer clear of the arguments, and we get on all right."

Nat thought of that as he walked around to the Knights of Columbus Hall that evening. Avoiding arguments was one thing he had learned to be good at. It was the principal way to stay out of trouble. He had done it by always having something else to do, but he didn't know how to use this with Cyrus. With others it was easy. When the signing party broke up, half a dozen guys wanted him to cruise around with them in somebody's car, but he told them he had to get back to the deli. Uncle Joe and Aunt Rose wanted to go bowling, and, besides, his brother might show up anytime.

"What brother?" they jeered. "When did you get a brother?" After he told them, they howled, "Six years! What was he in for?" Nat laughed and said nothing, wondering himself where his brother had been.

The nine o'clock crowd was still thick in the deli when Nat walked in. He began rolling up his sleeves before he reached the back entry and took his apron down. Both Rose and Joe worked behind the counter.

"Hey, Nat!" his uncle called out. "Tell this guy what kind a pizza we make here. He no come in before."

"The best in Boston," Nat said, while Aunt Rose tied his apron strings in back. She smoothed his shirt over his shoulder muscles.

"What'd I tell you?" Uncle Joe said. "Now, how do you like it?"

They worked side by side until the crowd thinned out. Only two or three groups were left in the booths sipping the last of their Pepsis, and only one man waited for a pizza to go when his uncle and aunt took off their aprons and went bowling. Nat wiped down the counters and scraped the crumbs from the grill. When the booths emptied, he carried the trash out in a huge buff-colored plastic bag and stuffed it into the Dempsey Dumpster in the alley. He came back to the stillness of the empty place, wiping the last booth as he passed.

The bells jingled, and he looked up. Instantly his stomach hardened. A man had come in. He was bearded and dirty and wore black motorcycle leather. Nat moved behind the counter, glancing swiftly through the window. It looked like only one big motorcycle out there. This biker must be alone, and, if he needed them, the biggest knives were on Nat's side.

"What can I do for you?" he asked.

The biker didn't reply. He glanced at Nat, flicked loose the rings on the chin strap and pulled the great silver-gray helmet away from his ears. He set it down on the counter and peeled his gloves. Then he scratched his beard under his chin where the strap rubbed, then his mustache, and then he ran his fingers through his hair. All the time he studied Nat. Their eyes met and locked. A sensation so intense flooded through Nat that sweat sprang from his scalp. The biker grinned a little and squinted and said, "Hi, Nat."

The pause that followed was long and empty. Nat was stunned into silence. His brother, Cyrus, had come back.

2
Another Way

Know something you can take with you.

— The Duke of the Road

"I never did learn how to make a pizza," Cyrus said, as he watched Nat filling the dough. He used both hands, pouring sauce with his right, sprinkling grated cheese with his left. "Aren't you overdoing it?"

Nat laughed. "This is a two-fifty special, with two-fifty in extras. You came a long way for a pizza." Nat slid the filled pastry from the wooden paddle onto the hot bottom shelf of the oven.

"That's not all I came for," his brother said.

A little shock of anxiety hit Nat. He was both eager and afraid to know why Cyrus had picked this moment to show up again.

"That's a Harley, isn't it, Cy?" Cyrus nodded. "It must have cost plenty."

"Not if you don't count my time. I picked it up cheap and rebuilt it."

"Where'd you learn to do that?"

"From the Duke," Cyrus said. "The Duke of the Road."

Nat went around the counter and sat down two stools away from Cy. "Did you come all the way across country on it?"

"Oh, yeh."

The smell of the pizza baking escaped through the cracks around the oven door and began to spread through the store. Cyrus unzipped his jacket and took a pack of cigarettes from his shirt pocket. He offered it to Nat, who shook his head.

"Athlete, hey?" Nat acknowledged it. "Any good?"

"Okay."

"Yeh? Get a letter? In what?"

"Football, basketball, baseball."

Cy exhaled a sigh of smoke. "That's okay, all right, but knowing how to make a pizza is better. Know something you can take with you, the Duke said, then you'll never be down and out. So when he handed me a wrench, I took it."

In the void of his brother's six mysterious years there were motorcycles and tools and someone called the Duke of the Road. Nat felt suddenly reticent about himself. He could think of nothing to equal whatever it was that mixed Cyrus with motorcycles and tools and the Duke and put him in command of his own life.

Cyrus rose a little from the stool and took his billfold from his hip pocket. It was so fat with money that it bulged open. Nat watched him deal out two tens and a five on the counter between them. "I took twenty-five from your drawer when I left," Cyrus said. He pushed the bills toward Nat.

For a minute Nat didn't move. One afternoon, six years before, he had come home from school to find Cy gone. His clothes were gone. An athletic bag from the Y was gone. His presence had flown from their bedroom. Suddenly Nat had thought of his money buried among his shirts and socks and scrabbled through a drawer. The money, too, had been gone. Then the vacant pit of his stomach began to fill with anger. There was no easy way to repair that time. Nat sat back, gripping his left wrist tightly in his right hand.

"Go ahead, take it. Don't be stupid."

Nat shook his head.

"Think of it as a graduation present." Cy laughed. Then he folded the bills and attempted to tuck them into Nat's shirt pocket. Nat shoved him away. Suddenly they were standing face to face, flushed and angry. "What the hell?"

"What the hell yourself." Nat bit his lip.

The bell on the pizza oven dinged. "Round One," Cy said. "Let's go back to our corners. You're going to have to tell me what that's all about."

Nat tucked the paddle under the pizza and drew it from the oven, slid it onto a tin and cut it into eighths. After pouring two Pepsis over ice, he went around the counter again and sat down. Cy watched him as he pulled a slice free of strings of cheese. "Forget it," Nat said. He slipped the bills into his pocket. "Thanks."

Cy watched him curiously, extracting sauce from his beard. "Where are Giuseppe and Rosie?"

"This is their bowling night."

Devouring the pizza, Cy seemed not to notice that Nat took only one slice. When he finished, he wiped his beard and mustache again. "We still sleeping in the same place? Help me roll that baby inside for the night."

Sitting on the dark street the motorcycle looked big. Once inside the deli it seemed twice the size. Nat held the door and pulled while Cy steadied and pushed from behind. By the time they had it inside on its stand, Nat had made some basic observations. It was a 900 cc Harley, metallic body and fairing, the windshield spattered with bugs, the headlamp glass cracked, the long black saddle slightly crushed where the rider sat, two rear-vision mirrors rising like an insect's antennae from the handlebars, the ribs of the cooling fins coated with grease and dust, metallic panniers sandwiching the rear wheel with a pack and a sleeping bag strapped across them. California plates.

"You ever ride one of these?"

"Nothing that big." In an instant Nat saw himself pulled up at a stoplight, his eyes hidden behind goggles, his head like a nut inside its helmet shell, his legs thrust out, the great bike vibrating beneath him. He felt something about to break out again.

"You ought to get one and come with me."

Following Cy up the back stairs to the little apartment above the deli, Nat tasted a loneliness as terrible and sudden as his anger. Cy didn't intend to stay. He was going on. They crossed the little overcrowded living room and went into the bedroom. Bunk beds almost filled the space, but a desk and a dresser and a set of bookshelves and a chair had been pushed in as well. By the time Nat pulled himself together, Cyrus had yanked off his boots, stripped off his shirt and leather pants, and climbed into the top bunk.

"Where are you going, Cyrus?"

"Right now? Maine, Vermont, New Hampshire — I've never seen this part of the country. Have you?"

"Me? Well, no, I mean yes. I've been to a few places for games."

"Did you see the place or did you stay in the gym?"

"Well, the gym, mostly."

"The locker room you mean. I mean where have you gone on your own?"

He didn't know how to tell someone who had been knocking around the world for six years that on his own he hadn't ventured often beyond the familiar part of the city.

"How much have you got, Nat? Joe been paying you?"

Nat murmured assent without admitting how much.

"I can show you how to fix up a bike and sell it for more than you paid for it at the end of the summer."

Nat felt the electric excitement, that pressure mounting against his habits, his instinct, but he said out loud, "I'll have to think about it. I was going to stay on in the deli until I picked up something better — you know . . ." His voice trailed off while the suggestion of adventure, experiences he'd never had, excited his thoughts. "I'd have to talk it over with Uncle Joe, too, I guess."

Cyrus laughed. "I haven't seen him for six years, but I know what he'll say. Hit the light, will you, man? I'm beat."

Nat flicked the switch and sat on the edge of the bed in the dark. Cy hadn't been there an hour, and already he was ripped in two. Stretching out on his back, he stared up at the bedsprings sagging under his brother's weight. "Damn you, Cyrus," he muttered. "Oh, hell, I don't know."

3

The Big
Blowup

No matter where you go,
don't forget you've been here.

— Aunt Rose's song

He slept better than he realized, because he hadn't heard the argument between Aunt Rose and Uncle Joe until Aunt Rose hissed, "Sh-sh-sh-sh-shhhhh." Then he got up, saw Cyrus still sound asleep on the upper bunk, and opened the door without a creak and went into the living room. Aunt Rose sat on the sofa in her hair rollers and robe, and Uncle Joe stood in the middle of the small room, shaking Cyrus's black leather jacket in his fist. He was about to say something when Nat appeared.

"What kinda brother is this?" His uncle lifted the jacket and gave it a shake. "What's this thing doing downstairs? I got to open the deli but no customers can get in. It smell like a garage."

"He's not what you think," Nat said, noticing that the heavy oil and gas odor had seeped upstairs.

"How you know?"

"Joe, you promised!" Aunt Rose cried out.

As Nat watched, his uncle's face altered from anger to discouragement. He gave the jacket a final halfhearted shake and dropped it on a chair. "I don't want to fight. I want it peace in here. I make it peace if I can watch my mouth."

"I think he's changed, Uncle Joe."

"How you tell? You talk to him one time. What do you know?"

"There you go again," Aunt Rose exclaimed. "You won't let him change, if you keep on like that."

His uncle sat down in his TV chair, and his shoulders slumped forward. He looked at Rose with a groan for help. "With Nat I got no trouble. With Cyrus I never say one right thing. So I promise to watch my mouth, but what good is that when I can't watch my head?"

"Think love," Aunt Rose said, "all the time."

"I try, but with Cyrus it don't come easy."

Nat wondered if he could ever bring himself to ask his uncle about buying a motorcycle and going with his brother. Anger would be down inside him somewhere, simmering on a back burner. At that moment Cyrus opened the bedroom door and came out. Instinctively, Nat stepped back as if to get out of the line of fire.

His uncle simply stared at him, while Aunt Rose burst into tears and threw herself into Cyrus's arms, weeping and crying out, "Look at him! Six years! Isn't he handsome? Even if he does have a beard and a lot of hair."

Laughing, Cyrus hugged her and said, "Rosie, you haven't changed a bit."

"Oh, and with my rollers still on! I forgot! Why didn't you two tell me I still had my rollers on? You knew I wanted to look right." She stood back, sobbing and laughing and looking at Cyrus.

Nat stirred uneasily. Cyrus had the same effect on the little apartment as the motorcycle had on the deli. The living room felt small and overcrowded with its figured wallpaper and print curtains and plastic flowers in cut-glass vases. He wondered how the place looked to his brother, and he noticed the little things, that the TV wasn't color and a dark spot stained the chair where Uncle Joe rested his head while he watched it.

Before the silence grew awkward, Aunt Rose asked, "Is that your — your whatchamacallit downstairs?"

"That's my motorcycle, Rose."

"Did you come all the way from California on it?"

"All the way."

"You didn't have any accidents?"

"None to speak of."

Before Nat could think of anything to fill the tense silence his uncle said, "What you mean, none to speak of?"

"It stopped once before I got off, that's what I mean." Cyrus tucked in his shirt while he glanced from Rose to Joe to Nat, and Nat felt certain that he considered saying something which he decided against. Rose watched anxiously while Joe seemed to harden for battle and then soften again. The crisis passed. Nat felt a wobble of relief.

That day Aunt Rose didn't go to work. Cyrus didn't come home after six years every day, she said, and they'd just have to wait to hear about him in the department store. When Cy rolled his motorcycle out of the shop to make room for the customers, he asked her if she'd like a ride around the block.

It gave Uncle Joe a start, and his face filled with anger again and he turned toward the back of the deli where Nat was stacking racks of glasses.

Cyrus settled onto his machine and Aunt Rose got on behind him and hung on around his waist for her life, laying her cheek against the leather of his jacket and squeezing her eyes shut. Cy laughed and urged her to relax. She opened her eyes just once to see the pavement, concrete and asphalt and old brick patches, whiz beneath her gaze. By the time they reached the square, she sat up straight. When he saw her, Officer Flanagan held back the Saturday traffic for them, and she let go with one hand long enough to give him a wave. Coming down the one-way street to the deli, she began to laugh with excitement, and her face flushed and her hair flew out behind her.

"She look like when I first met her," Joe said, watching through the window. "She like excitement. I forget that."

Nat knew the sides were shifting.

On Sunday Uncle Joe wanted to take them out to the beach. Nat worried a little that the old Dodge sedan wouldn't be good enough for Cyrus, but Cy didn't say anything scornful about it. When they got to the seashore parking lot, Cy took out his billfold to pay the fee, and everyone stared in silence as it bulged open. Uncle Joe stiffened and asked, "Where you get so much money?" and Cyrus replied, "It wasn't easy."

"You no steal —"

Nat's body tightened like a fist.

"I no steal, Uncle Giuseppe."

Nat relaxed, realizing that Cyrus had changed. Six years

ago he had yelled at Uncle Joe, "Every time I get my hands on five bucks, you think I stole it. You want me to steal it? Do you? Push me and I will." Now he half grinned and glanced sideways at Nat, saying, "This uncle of ours, he's just the same."

"I mean okay." Joe looked discouraged and Nat felt his hurt.

They spread out the beach blanket and set down the picnic cooler. While Aunt Rose waded up to her ankles, they made one wild dash into the cold surf and came out again.

"It's warmer in California," Cyrus said.

They sailed the Frisbee around, the three of them.

"You're still built good," Uncle Joe said. "Not too much beer or sitting around yet."

Cyrus laughed. "In California we work out on the beach a lot." He pressed one bicep hard against his chest, and the muscle spread and tightened. "You look all right, Nat." He gave him an admiring inspection which made Nat smirk with pleasure.

"He letter in three sports this year," Uncle Joe said, and Aunt Rose called from the blanket, "I had to give up my bingo night to get to all the games."

"She'd do anything for Nat," Uncle Joe said. "For you, too, when you was here."

Girls unfurling their beach towels nearby smiled at Cyrus, who acknowledged them impersonally. Nat wondered if he had a girl out in California, or if he had a dozen girls, one indistinguishable from another. There was so much he didn't know about Cyrus, and if he knew more, he wondered what he would think. He hadn't dated much himself for almost two years now, not since his girl had cut him off because he didn't call her every night. He had to study and then spent the weekends with the team and working in the deli. He missed her for a while, particularly when he saw her with somebody else, but half the time she had made him miserable and anxious and he didn't miss that.

When the fog rolled in and the sand grew cold under the gray billows, Rose and Joe wandered up the beach looking for stones and shells. Nat pulled on his sweatshirt while Cyrus watched the girls roll up their towels and depart. He propped his head on a driftwood log and, still watching them, he said, "Nat, what do you think about getting a bike and coming with me?"

Nat took his brother in. Their eyes met, and he felt a force like an undertow pulling him after Cyrus, eating away the sand beneath the decisions holding up his life. Then Cyrus laughed, and his eyes twinkled, and he said, "Why not?"

Suddenly Nat felt awfully good and he laughed with him and he knew without being told that whatever Cyrus had been doing in the last six years, he was on top of it. "Why not?" he said.

Then he thought of his uncle. His mind clouded over just as the sky over the dunes had done and he added, "I have to talk it over with Uncle Joe. I can't just — you know — tell him."

Cyrus shrugged and said, "Okay — you handle it," and didn't mention it again.

He found handling it next to impossible. The first time that he and Uncle Joe were alone in the deli Nat wondered how to open the subject. He scraped chopped onions into a stainless steel container and began washing green peppers in the sink. Joe passed behind him, carrying a rack of glasses. "Oh, do they smell good, eh, Nat? Fresh bread, onions, they smell good, but green pepper — they are best!" Nat opened the sausage and waved it under his uncle's nose, and they laughed.

A moment later Uncle Joe said, "What'sa matter, Nat? Your brother got you bothered?"

"He wants me to take the summer off and go traveling with him." Nat watched his uncle.

"You want to go?" His uncle glanced at him. "You want to go." The glasses clinked against the metal rack as he put it under the counter. "You get to know your own brother, and that's good. That's the way it should be. And you got the money, Nat. You work all the time, in school, after school for the sports. Maybe you need little vacation." He opened a box of furry paper plates for the pizzas. "I can get along okay. Lonesome, but okay."

Nat's throat lumped and his eyes stung, and he worked his lips to control his feelings. Uncle Joe laughed and put his arms around him and patted him on the back and said, "You got a brother. Get to know him. Go see the world. I give you my blessing. Just don't go on no bike."

Nat stiffened in his uncle's embrace. As Uncle Joe took his shoulders in his hands and held him off, he said, "You was planning to go on that bike."

Then Uncle Joe was yelling, "No! Nat, no!" and he was yelling, "I wasn't going to ride on behind!" and trying to explain until he heard Aunt Rose clatter down the back stairs and run into the store, crying out, "For God's sake, what's happening down here?" But she couldn't understand with the two of them yelling at once.

She picked up the paper napkin holder and banged it down

on the counter. "Shut up! Both of you! Joe, you're white as your apron. You'll have a coronary if you don't get the blood going around. What's the matter with you two? Nat, put down that knife."

"I was going to chop the peppers."

"I know that. What are you two arguing about?"

His uncle drew a deep breath. "He wants to go traveling with his brother, and I say okay but not on no bike. He wants to go on a bike." He looked helplessly at Rose.

"I wasn't going to ride on behind, Aunt Rose. Cy says he knows enough about bikes to get one for me and fix it up so I can sell it for more than I paid for it at the end of the summer."

"Maybe by the end of the summer it's in the junkyard and you're in the graveyard. Everybody fixed up good then."

"Kids get killed playing Little League. Two guys got wiped out a couple of weeks ago when their car hit the supports under the expressway." Nat was yelling again. "Something can happen right here."

"While you live, you take a risk," Uncle Joe yelled, "but four wheels and a body is better."

"Cyrus has been riding for almost six years," Aunt Rose said, "and he —"

Uncle Joe yelled at her, "Whose side you take, Rosie?" Chewing her lips, she glared back at him. He lowered his voice. "We don't know nothing about this Cyrus. Maybe he's a Devil's Angel — how do we know?"

"I don't think he's a Hell's Angel, Uncle Joe."

His uncle shrugged. "We got no proof." He studied one side of a green pepper, then the other, and glanced at Rose. "I don't know. Rose, what you think?"

24   *Into the Road*

Nat and his uncle looked across the counter at Aunt Rose. She sat on the stool with her eyes fixed in distance.

"What did you do when you were eighteen, Joe?"

Joe studied the green pepper. "That's when I went to sea on the fishing boats." The glance he gave Rose was more helpless than before.

"Did your father want you to?"

"He no like it, but what could he do? I was going."

Aunt Rose nodded. "That's the way you feel when you're eighteen."

Joe frowned, gave Rose a dirty look, threw down the pepper and split it with the knife. "How about me? How about the work here in the deli? I thought you was going to stick around till something big came up — maybe assistant chef someplace?"

"He'll be back," Aunt Rose said.

Uncle Joe sighed. He continued chopping the pepper. Nat smiled and put his arms around his uncle, who remained stiff and unyielding in his embrace and gave him a dark look of reproach and helplessness and love while he muttered, "I give my blessing. What else can I do?"

4

Learning
the Process

Count on it — a biker leaves a lot of skin.

— Ruckus

Now the final two weeks of school took on a breathless, nervous quality. Something new was coming. The doors inside him cracked open. Nat felt a kind of electricity surging through him whenever he came to rest momentarily, teetering on the curb, staring into his dark empty school locker. The old familiar days were running out.

"You ever ride a bike?" Cyrus asked, sitting back in Uncle Joe's chair, drinking a beer and watching the Merv Griffin show.

"Yeh, a couple of times. We rented 125s one day out at Hampton Beach, and some guys let me ride theirs a few times. Why?"

"You ought to know as much as possible before you set out on the street."

"How about riding yours?"

"Not on your life," Cy said.

"How'm I going to get all this experience then?"

Cy scrooched down, absorbed in the TV, and belched. Anger sang through Nat.

The next day he went around to the branch library off Orient Square and found Miss Lionetta behind the dark mahogany desk. He hadn't been her size since the sixth grade.

"Why, hello, Nat." Her eye glasses glittered as she turned her face upward. "Long time no see, and so on. Something must be on your mind."

"I'm kind of thinking about motorcycles, Miss Lionetta."

"Oh-oh."

"And I want to know as much as I can before I make the move. Do you have anything I can read or — ?"

"Oh, have I! It just came in. I've had it on order. It's called *Bike Fever* by Lee Gutkind. Isn't that a moniker for you for a motorcyclist? It's right there on the New Book shelf."

Sitting at the old, dark table, Nat leafed through the book. He browsed here and there until he came to Chapter Seventeen. There he read:

Memorize the machine first . . . the cyclist must learn to read the controls without seeing them. . . . Push the bike to its center stand and begin: The handlebar grip on the right-hand side is actually the throttle. It serves the same purpose as a gas pedal on an automobile. Your bike accelerates as you turn the grip toward you. When turned the other way, speed is reduced. The lever right above the left grip is the clutch. You must squeeze that lever every time you shift gears. If you hook your heels firmly on the footpegs, the gear shift lever will be right above your left toe . . . there's a small green spot on your speedometer that lights up in neutral position. Starting from there, you push the shifting lever down with your toe to go into first gear. As you pick up speed, you lift the lever up one notch with your toe. Now, you're in second. Then higher one notch for third. Still higher for fourth and even higher for fifth gear. Each time, before you change gears, you squeeze the clutch.

Then there was a paragraph about variations in makes, some with different gear patterns and more speeds than others and a bit about electric starters.

Learn how to start the hard way first . . . standardize the starting procedure. Do it the same way all the time so you don't forget any of the steps. Turn on the gas — fuel must be manually activated for a motorcycle. Look in the manual to find out where the fuel petcock is. Turn on the ignition and make sure the cycle is in neutral. Press lightly on your kick start pedal and open your throttle slightly. Then throw your weight on the kick starter, kick down as if you are trying to smash the pavement . . . with the machine started, let the kick starter up slowly. Don't let it snap up or you'll wear out the starting mechanism.

Now, begin moving:

Squeeze the clutch lever closed. Shift into first gear. Then simultaneously and slowly, increase throttle speed and release the clutch lever. Then stop and start again. When the engine stalls, you haven't fed it enough gas. When you take off too rapidly, you're feeding too much gas. When it bucks forward, you're letting the clutch out too quickly. Squeeze in the clutch before stopping because that action deactivates the rear wheel, the main power generator. Increase speed after a while, just enough to shift into the higher gears. The owner's manual will tell at which speeds to shift to second, third, fourth, and fifth.

And to brake:

In any situation, there is only one way to stop: quickly squeeze the clutch lever to disengage the clutch, shut down the throttle, push on your rear brake pedal first, then squeeze your front brake lever. This process must be accomplished almost, but not quite, simultaneously. Always use both brakes. Neither is strong enough to safely control the weight of the rider, let alone a machine with both rider and passenger. Neither provides a secure balance. Squeezing only the front brake might lock the front wheel, which can cause the rider to fly over the handlebars. If you use the back brake alone, the cycle could fishtail. The brakes are designed to be effective together. At 50 miles per hour, a cycle, braked correctly, needs 175 feet to stop. An automobile needs 243. Since you brake from the rear first, many riders get in the habit of relying wholly on the rear brake. But both brakes must be used for maximum efficiency. Adding the front brake increases stopping capacity by 70 percent.

In an automobile with a standard transmission, you can come to a stop in any gear. But motorcycle transmissions are not designed that way. Even if they were, part of the skill of riding a motorcycle is being in the right gear at the right time. Often the margin of safety is contingent on how quickly the cyclist can avoid a dangerous situation. So the cycle must have a potential power spurt at all times. Which means that downshifting is important when coming to a stop.

If you are going 25 miles per hour in third gear while accelerating, then while decelerating you should be in third gear when moving at approximately the same speed. Since you are riding in lower, more controllable gears when downshifting, remember that your engine must work harder to maintain speed. So the rider must feed a little more gas each time he is downshifting. The process is simple.

We are riding at 40 miles per hour in fourth gear. We see a stop sign ahead. We slow down to 30 and shift into third gear, opening our throttle just enough so that our engine speed (rpms) is high enough to match the road speed. We slow down to 20 and repeat the process. The gears are slowing us down, not the brakes. When we stop at the sign we shift into neutral and wait until we can move forward. We should not shift into neutral too early for we lose the possibility of acceleration if needed.

Learn to use the gears. Downshift to gain additional power while climbing a hill. Merely feeding more gas in a high gear will not do the job and will put unnecessary strain on the engine. But never downshift into a speed higher than the maximum allowed in a gear as outlined in the owner's manual.

On handling corners:

As you approach the curve, slow down until you are a little bit below the speed you need to safely make it. You'll learn this with experience and practice, but in the beginning be overcautious. Go slower than you need to. Make sure you are in a gear that will allow you to accelerate out of the turn. If you have to downshift to reach the gear, do that before the turn, not during it. Downshifting in a turn might unsettle your balance.

The best advice I can give you is to not turn too sharply. Try to go into the turn wide, and come out of it a little more than half a lane's width from oncoming traffic when the turn is completed.

But still, there's a difference between making a left and a right turn. When making a right, even though you are driving on the right, you should ease out toward the left-hand center of the lane. Then lean. That should put you in about the middle of the road you are turning into. But if you start too close to the right-hand edge of the road, you could lean too hard and smash into the curb. Or not lean hard enough and drift into the opposite lane. By beginning a little over to the left, a margin for error remains.

You should make a left, however, from the left-hand side of the lane because, in this case, you are banking away from oncoming traffic and you need ample drifting room so you don't crash into the curb.

Ride defensively, Gutkind wrote:

Watch the eyes of motorists when you can or the front wheels when you're passing a car, or the wheels of cars in oncoming traffic when you're passing an intersection where they could turn. Assume you are invisible to the motorist. He can't see you. You don't know what he's going to do, but you do know that he doesn't see you. Develop a paranoia. Expect every automobile door you pass to open right into your gut. Remember that all motorists are blind and crazy. You can count on them only to do the unexpected.

And incidentally, keep in the left half of the lane whenever you're riding. Then, if the car behind you wants to pass, he's got to go in the opposite lane to do it. Otherwise, with you too far to the right, he might decide to try to squeeze in beside you. And if there's any oil dripped from trucks or cars on the road, it should be right in the middle. That's the slipperiest part of the road.

And don't let cars intimidate you. Hold your position on the road.

If you go down, and sooner or later you will:

Usually it happens so quickly that there's very little you can do. Of course, if you see a car coming right at your head or leg, then sure, get the hell out of the way. Jump off. But at high speeds, things will happen too fast. Besides, in those situations, you will doubtless be knocked off the machine. Your best bet then is to tuck yourself into a ball and roll to the ground. Don't try to break your fall with your hands, or you'll break them.

At slow speeds or in heavy traffic, try staying with your machine. Jumping free might put you right in front of a moving car. At least with your bike you have more visibility and weight. And more protection. You won't be dragged very far at 20 or 25 miles per hour either. The bike will stop soon after it makes contact with the road surface.

Finally, Gutkind said:

The way to learn to ride a motorcycle is from the beginning. Slowly. And with patience. There are no alternatives or exceptions. That is the only way to be fairly certain of staying alive.

Nat closed the book, thinking, it's scary — and exciting — and — . He studied the cover picture of Gutkind astride his BMW looking over his shoulder. And he laughed.

Miss Lionetta's glasses glittered as she looked up at him. "What do you think, Nat? I think I could ride one out of here myself after reading that."

"You could." He laughed again. Standing on the library steps, he felt one of those breathless moments — doors opening — teetering on the edge.

5

Telling
a Dog

In this business the machine's got to fit the man —
and the man's got to fit the machine — no other way.

— The Duke

Cyrus spread out the Sunday paper's want ad–section on the
floor between his feet and leaning his forearms on his knees
surveyed it. His face took on a greater intensity, his eyes
bright and sharp.

"The motorcycle shop won't be open until tomorrow," Nat
said. "We can't do much till then."

"That's one place we aren't goin'," Cyrus said.

"They've got the bikes," Nat said.

"They've got the prices, too. If you mean to come out ahead
on this, we are goin' to have to deal tight."

Lying on the rug, Nat rolled over and propped his head on
his hand. "But I can't buy a Harley like yours, and you told
me yourself it took you six months to rebuild it."

Cy glanced up, his eyes narrowed and gleaming. "Maybe
you can. We'll see about that." Then he returned to studying
the want ads.

Nat sat up and scanned the narrow column of type under

the heading "Motorcycles." "How about this one? '1970 Harley-Davidson, full dress $3000 or best offer'?"

"Well, skip that," Cyrus laughed. "But it's probably worth it. Tell me what you think of this one: '1968 BMW R60, white, rebuilt engine, excellent condition, asking $1100.' "

While his brother watched him, Nat considered. "That's a good make."

Cyrus nodded.

"It's a touring bike, which is what we're looking for."

"Right."

"But it's already been rebuilt so we'd be paying for someone else's work and parts and everything."

Cyrus's face seemed to glow briefly, and Nat felt the warmth. He was learning. "What else?" his brother asked.

"I don't know. I can't see much more."

"It's pretty old even for a good bike like that. It might be worth it, but it's out of our price range anyway. Here's a three-year-old, 450 ccs, 3,800 miles. $900 firm."

"That's pretty high, Cy."

"He may not mean it. That one's worth a look."

"How about this one: 'Female must sell one-year-old 250 cc, 3,600 miles, excellent condition, many extras, $795.'?"

"Two fifty is a little light." Cyrus considered. "But I'd like to see the chick who's got it. Circle that one."

In the end Nat had drawn lines around seven ads. After calling the telephone numbers, he had reduced the list to five. One had sold and another didn't answer. It surprised Nat when Cy asked Uncle Joe if he could borrow his car, and he asked, "Why not ride your bike?"

"No use alerting them that we know anything." Cy

laughed, his eyes glinting, and Nat caught the excitement. Watching him, Uncle Joe said, "You make me think of my own uncle in the old country. He traded donkeys, and just before he begin to bargain, his eyes look like that."

Cy laughed with relish. "Somehow it got in the blood."

He squeezed his uncle's shoulder, and Uncle Joe looked deeply pleased. He's coming from where the blood ties are made, Nat thought, and he felt the kind of affectionate ache he often did for his uncle.

The folded newspaper rested on his knees as Nat rode beside his brother and watched out the window for the street numbers.

"What the hell street are we on?" Cyrus complained. "Doesn't this town put up signs for anything but cross streets?"

"You're supposed to know what you're on," Nat said. "Beantown's always been this way."

"I never noticed that before. Man, the trees are really big back here."

A great maple six feet thick, the heavy bark almost breaking from the trunk, hung over the street. Behind it a three-flat wooden building occupied most of the ground. "That's it, Cy. There's the bike in the drive. You do the talking."

Cy nodded; his eyes already narrowed, taking the inventory, weighing, judging. They parked the car at the curb and strolled up the drive. They stood a few feet from the motorcycle and looked at it. Then, quickly, Cy leaned down and laid his hand on the cylinder cooling fins. At that moment a side door opened, and the owner stepped out of the house.

"We're the guys who called," Nat grinned.

"A lot of guys have called." The man wore a dirty green

T-shirt, and he held a can of beer in one hand. He didn't smile as Cy kept his hand on the cooling fins without looking up, then squatted beside the rear wheel, ran his fingers around the rim and felt the tire's tread. Then carefully, as if he weighed it, he lifted the drive chain two or three times. He stood up and moved behind the bike and sighted it lengthwise. As he walked around it, he pressed down on the seat, glanced at the speedometer and down at the kick starter. The owner said, "Take a test ride if you want."

"We aren't interested."

The man shrugged, growling, "Don't waste my time, then," and turned back to the door.

"Thanks, anyway," Nat called as he followed his brother down the drive to the car. They got in, slammed the doors, and drove off before Nat spoke. "What did you find? It looked all right to me. It was pretty clean."

"It's been in a wreck," Cy said. He pulled into a drive-in and ordered two large root beers in frosted mugs and paid no attention to the girl who brought them. "Something was wrong the way it stood on its stand. You know, just not quite — true. Then he'd warmed it up. Maybe he just went out for something, but maybe he wanted to cover up. The rear rim is bent, and the whole back end doesn't line up with the front. That machine has been in a smash, and it's a hell of a lot older than the speedometer reading. The chain was very slack. If that guy hadn't stepped out, I could have given you his description from the bike: a rough hand, cleaned it up for sale but didn't bother to take care of it. He thought we wouldn't see."

Nat grinned. "Where'd you learn all that, Cy? My gosh, you really know these machines."

Cy wiped foam from his mustache with the back of his hand. "There isn't anything mysterious about it. You just have to read the machine. You have to learn the signs — you know what I mean? You can't take the engine out and look at it. But there are things you can see, some on the bike and some on the owner. Where do we go next? I'm just getting warmed up."

While Nat ran his fingers down the want ad column, his brother took a long swallow and said, "I hate guys like that."

Nat looked up, surprised at the strength of his feelings. "That guy with the bike?"

"Yeh, that guy. I despise him." Cyrus finished the root beer and set the mug down on the window tray. "He had a beautiful piece of machinery in his hands, and he killed it. He abused it. He beat it up. The beauty of a motorcycle is the delicacy of the way it works."

"Delicacy?" Nat repeated, his surprise growing into astonishment.

"Delicacy." Cyrus stressed the word. "I don't mean the parts. They're tough all right. It's the balance, you know, the relationships. A bike's not a Mack truck. There's not a whole lot of margin. It's more like a watch. If you tromp on it, it'll stay tromped." He laughed, and Nat studied his brother's bearded face, wondering about the world his brother had wandered in and arrested by the shining fragments of knowledge he had learned there.

They drove back and forth over several streets but could not locate the second one on the list. The third was easier. The kid's precise directions were just that. As they pulled up in front of the large brick house set back in its trimmed evergreens and laurels, Nat had a moment of embarrassment for the faded blue Dodge.

"What do you think?" Cyrus asked.

"He doesn't hurt for money," Nat murmured.

"Now you're reading signs."

When the kid answered the front door, he was dirtier than the first man. A piece of the American flag was stitched across the seat of his jeans, and his hair hung in greasy waves over his shoulders. "We came about the bike," Nat said. The kid grunted, and stuffing his hands in what was left of his pockets, he led them around to the attached garage. He threw up the overhead door and said, "The black one."

Spread across half the garage were three motorcycles, an old dirt bike, an absolutely brand new metallic green moto-cross bike, and an older, larger bike, a BMW 500. The kid mumbled something and stood back.

This time Cyrus led Nat through the complete list of checkpoints he held in his mind. The machine was cold. There was no chain to worry about. The frame was true and although it had some scratches and dents, it showed no signs of a major crash. The wear and tear on the foot-pegs and kick starter and shift lever correlated to the speedometer reading. Cy and Nat stood back to consider, while the kid stood in the open doorway, hanging his head and shuffling his bare feet awkwardly.

"How about a test ride?" Cyrus asked. The kid mumbled and shuffled and handed him the key. Cy rolled the bike out of the garage, allowed a little gasoline to flow into the car-buretor, checked the brake levers, and stepped down hard on the kick starter. Nothing happened. The kid stirred. Cy stepped down again and then again and looked at him.

The kid seemed to come to life. "Got a kind of quirk — I mean —" he said, took Cyrus's place beside the bike, did something Nat couldn't detect but which made Cyrus laugh, stepped on the starter and brought on a roar. He gave Cy a halfway grin as he turned the bike over to him. "What's the gear pattern?" "One down and three up." Cy rode down the drive and disappeared. Nat heard a tappet noise in the motor. He stood silently with the tongue-tied owner, first sticking his fingers in his hip pockets, then crossing his arms on his chest, glancing around the garage at the workbench with its tools, the extra helmets hanging in a row, a little pyramid of oil cans underneath. "You're really into bikes."

The kid grinned a little.

"You do your own repair?"

The kid nodded. "Tune-up — change the oil — top-end overhaul, that's all." Nat nodded, and the kid nodded, and they were still nodding back and forth when Cyrus returned. While he flicked on the light and tested the horn, he said, "It'll take a lot of work to clear up that tappet noise." He tried to start the engine again and it wouldn't start. "And that little quirk doesn't go away even when it's warmed up." He turned to Nat. "I don't know if we've got the man-hours between us. What're you asking — five hundred?"

"Well — I was thinking — I put in the paper — I don't know — about nine, I guess."

Cyrus whistled. "Six is more like it." He pulled the bike back on its stand. "Well, we'll think about it. Thanks a lot. If we're interested after looking over some others, we'll let you know." The brothers strolled down the drive, got into the faded blue sedan and drove away. Nat gave the kid a final wave before they disappeared.

"What did you think?" Nat asked.

"A BM for less than nine! That's coming close. And he doesn't know how to dicker." Cy licked his lips, pulled on his nose and stroked his mustache with his thumb and first finger. "What's next?"

"Next is Female must sell."

"Ah-ha. Show me the way."

The girl was in the parking lot beside a rambling old apartment building. In bike boots and yellow buckskin pants, a bright green helmet and buckskin jacket, she sat astride a red Honda 500 while a FOR SALE sign was propped on the fork of a smaller bike. She watched as the brothers pulled up, parked, and strolled toward her. Cyrus made a low rumbling in his throat which only Nat could hear.

"I was about to leave. I thought you guys weren't coming." She unsnapped the helmet, eased it from her head and shook her long reddish hair free. It rippled like a fishing net being thrown out, and Nat almost exclaimed aloud. Cy kept his eye on the bikes as if nothing could distract him from the mission. When he had gone through the checkpoints, he stood back and considered.

"I'll be honest with you," the girl said. "I need the money to meet the payment on this one, and I want to get out of this town. Otherwise, I wouldn't have gone for a big bike."

"Who took care of it for you?" Cy asked.

"The dealer maintained it. I always took it back to them. Oh, I changed the oil, but that's all."

"Why didn't you trade it in?"

"I thought I could get more for it selling it myself."

"Helmet and lock and chain go with it?"

"No, I need those for my new bike and I'm keeping this

helmet for my grandchildren." She stroke the smooth green fiberglass, licked one fingertip and polished the block letters that read MS. AMERICA across the back.

"Six hundred is about as high as we can go," Cy said.

"I'm asking $795," the girl said, and her voice was hard. "But I'll be honest with you. Seven and a quarter is my best offer so far. I'm not going to do anybody a favor and go lower."

"We've got another one for less. It'll take some reworking, but we can do it."

"All right," the girl said. "I'll be honest with you. I was lying. My best offer has been $695."

Nat saw his savings halved in a stroke, and his nervousness rose again. Cyrus was very free with someone else's money, but in the end he didn't make an offer. She wouldn't come down, and besides, 250 cc was underpowered. They fell to talking about touring.

"Five hundred is a big bike for a woman," Cyrus said. "And that Honda's pretty sporty."

"It reminds me of the horse I used to have at home, terrific looking, big and strong and well-behaved."

Instinctively Nat tried to exude those qualities while Cy said, "Not very exciting, but all right." A question seemed to grow on the girl's face.

"Maybe we'll see you on the road," Nat said.

"That'd be great!" she said. "How will I know you?"

"Well, Cyrus has California plates on an old Harley-Davidson. I don't know what I'll be on yet."

"If you see a green helmet that says Ms. America, I'm inside it. Keep in touch." She dazzled Nat with a smile while Cyrus stroked his mustache.

Their fifth call turned out to be like the first, a machine much the worse for wear and an owner who was bad news. The bike had gone through several hands and looked it.

"Too much work," Cyrus murmured after a brief appraisal, and Nat realized suddenly that he had made the same assessment. He was learning. He knew how to tell a dog when he saw one.

For a week they read the classified ads in the daily papers and the neighborhood weekly, and several times they borrowed their uncle's car to follow an item through. Cy kept a complete file in his head. He knew where they had seen any given bike, what the owner was like, the pros and cons of the bike's condition without depending on notes of any kind. Each one had something going for it and something against it. "It's a matter of finding the one with the damages we can do something about," Cyrus said.

"Ms. America's bike looked pretty good to me."

"It was, but we'll never get her down and she shouldn't. There just isn't that much to fix. She doesn't come with it, anyway."

In the end they went back to the kid with the three machines in the double garage. Cy offered him $625 while the kid shuffled and mumbled and said he kind of wanted $850. Cy pointed out some obvious repairs and what they'd be likely to cost, and the kid said, "Well, $825." Nat looked out the garage door chewing his lower lip and tried to think about mowing that lawn and trimming around the flower beds. Cy said he couldn't see more than $750 because of the clicking noise deep in the engine, might be the timing chain. Then the kid said, "Would $775 sound all right," as if Cy were doing him a favor, and Cy replied in a tone of generosity that it would be just fine.

With that Cy gave Nat a quick glance, and Nat pulled out his billfold. Being careful that he held it so that the kid couldn't see that he had brought more than that, he counted out $775. For another ten dollars he bought one of the kid's helmets. The little layered stack of green on the edge of the workbench gave Nat second thoughts as he remembered the hours it took to earn it. While the kid made out a receipt on a piece of smudged paper and found the title and vehicle registration, a minor state of shock gripped Nat. What have I done? he wondered, I'm out $785, and I'm in a piece of machinery I don't even know how to run.

They stood around for a few minutes, and Cy and the kid, whose name was Tookie Hillman, talked bike racing. Tookie had been racing motocross for a year, trying to win points to move from novice rating to amateur, the next higher rank. Now he had his new bike, he said, he just might make it. "What you guys going to do?"

"We're hittin' the road." Cy grinned, fastening the helmet.

"Come on to the next race — be big — up in Maine — Rumney."

"You going to be there?"

The kid grinned and nodded. "Me — and the bike."

"See ya there maybe. Come on, Nat, lead off in that Dodge, will you? I'll never find my way across Beantown in a million years."

The kid looked at him in surprise. "You aren't going to ride it?"

"I don't have bikes on my driver's license yet," Nat said, which was true but only the half of it. He drove off before Tookie could ask anything more.

〰6〰
The Fixers

When everything's out where you can
get at it, that's half the battle.

— The Duke

Cy's feet hung down from the upper bunk the next morning when Nat tried to get his eyelids apart. They had watched the late movie on TV and then watched another that started at one A.M. It felt as if he had just crawled into bed, and the movie was so bad he wondered why he had sat through it, not to mention all the commercials for used cars and sofa beds and fifties rock 'n' roll records.

"Come on. Out," Cy said, jumping down and hitting the floor so hard that the building shook. Nat groaned. Cy ripped off the top sheet. "This is it!" He pulled on his pants and went out.

For a few minutes Nat lay on the bed, thinking that he had looked forward, anticipated getting out of high school just to lie in bed late any and every morning he felt like it, and no sooner had the time come than a spoiler had come with it. Already it was too late to do anything. He was committed. He got up, pulled on his blue jeans, put a piece of bread down the toaster while he poured a bowl of cereal. Then he carrried them downstairs.

Behind the deli there was a wide place in the alley. The deli building and its nearest neighbor weren't as deep as the others around them, which left the brick paved open space where Aunt Rose had a few boxes of petunias baking in the sun beside the back door, and the Dempsey Dumpster container stood by the alley. In a storage shed which was once an icehouse Cyrus set up his repair shop. He had swept the old dirt floor clean.

Sleepily Nat sat down on the back step and watched. His newly purchased BMW stood on its stand in a puddle of water near the adjacent building. Cy had hosed it down. Now he moved it into the icehouse. Aunt Rose had given Cy an old oversized bath towel, which he spread out beside the bike. With a wrench Cy removed the valve cover on the right-hand cylinder and laid it in the upper left-hand corner of the towel. With a felt-tip pen he marked it #1. Suddenly awake, Nat watched closely. Cy's eyes were sharp and intent, and although his beard disguised his face, Nat felt certain it, too, had sharpened intently.

After Cyrus laid part by part out in a row following the sequence in which he took them off the bike, he marked each one by number and by function, using the felt-tip pen on the white towel. After a while he glanced up at Nat, grinned, and asked, "See what I'm doin'?"

"You're laying it all out in order."

"You always use the same order, left to right, the way you read, so you can't forget how you laid them out. When you reassemble, you reverse the order, bottom row right to left, then next to bottom row from the right over. The numbers are double insurance. You always check which number you're working on. That way you cut down the chances of skipping over a part and finding it lying there all by itself when you're done."

"Does that happen to you anymore?"

Cy sat back on his heels, grinning. "That happens to everybody just often enough to remind you to keep your mind on what you're doin'. Is there any coffee up there? Are you as good with eggs as you are with a pizza?"

"If I go upstairs, I'll miss out on what you're doing."

"I won't get that far, not on an empty stomach. Besides, I've got to read the manual. I've never worked on a BM before."

After he fixed breakfast for Cyrus in the apartment upstairs, Nat brought it down and sat on the step while he ate.

"How'd you get in with the Duke of the Road, Cy?"

"I didn't get in with him." Cy pushed a bite into his cheek. "I got turned over to him."

Nat's stomach tightened. He got up and closed the door. "By the cops?"

"By the court. That twenty-five of yours didn't go too far."

"Was the Duke a probation officer?"

Cy held out his hand, little finger and thumb extended, and rocked it. "Kind of a one-man halfway house. The judge said that or jail so I took that." He went back to the machine and knelt beside it.

Nat bit his fingernail, thinking what to ask next. Cy fell to work again and didn't speak, didn't seem to hear, and Nat was left curious and apprehensive.

He stayed until the late morning crowd began to come into the deli and Uncle Joe needed him. About two it had thinned out, and he took Cy a sub and a pint of milk and a packet of potato chips and sat on the step with the door behind him closed now. He could hear when his uncle wanted him, but Uncle Joe couldn't hear them.

"What you get caught stealing?"

Examining a screw for stripped threads. Cy didn't answer for a minute. "Hubcaps." He smiled a little wryly. "I was livin' off the street, and then the court offered me board and room with this guy Duke Rhoades, so I took it. I figured I didn't have to take him too seriously. I was two months to eighteen — then I'd just disappear. I'd know L.A. by then." Cy sat back on his heels. "So the judge calls up the Duke. I nearly swallowed my eyeballs. He's about six four, ex-marine, ex-linebacker, ex-con. This guy could handle six of us like nothin'. The first thing he says is, 'You're goin' straight from now on,' and when he says straight, he means straight. He'd make Uncle Joe look like the godfather."

Cy wiped his hands on a greasy rag, laughing. "The first night he says, 'You can start in the shop in the morning.' I was too nervous and scared to ask what shop. So the next day we go to the shop. It has a big sign — THE DUKE OF THE ROAD — HARLEY-DAVIDSON SALES AND SERVICE — ALSO LESSER MAKES. And this shop is neat as a pin. I looked around and thought, jeese, this guy's a regular old maid. I'm going to have to dust the parts boxes, and I did, too. From hubcaps to Harleys is farther than you think."

Cy bent over the machine in silence for a while, and Nat reflected on his brother's story. "You must have gone from the parts department to the shop somewhere along the line."

"Yeh, after a while I graduated. I didn't like it at first. In Parts you saw everybody, and everybody came in there — the old guys who'd been ridin' bikes since 1915, stunt men from the movies, Hell's Angels, Momma Grabowski, the cops — everybody."

"But mechanic's pay must have been better."

"You'd better believe. But I earned it. The Duke was dead serious, especially about machines." He blew into an empty slot. "I was tryin' to fix something one day, and I couldn't do it right, so after tryin' about ten times, I figured out a way around it. When the Duke saw that, he sort of swelled up with rage, not at me exactly but at the insult to the machine. He took my tools away from me and did it right. Made me watch. That's the kind of guy he is." Cy fell silent again as he worked.

7

A Little Help from Some Friends

There are places to come from, and places to go.

— Joni Mitchell

When word got around, Nat's friends began to cruise down the alley and pull in to see how things were going. Cy needed a stool to sit on as he worked, and a kid who worked on the fish pier brought over two codfish crates, one for each side of the bike. After a while the fish smell went away, and they were perfect. Sometimes the deli customers stepped out in back while they waited for their pizza. A machinist took a couple of parts that had to be either machined or replaced and brought them back the next day. Uncle Joe made him a pizza free. "That's squid pro quo," Aunt Rose said, and they agreed.

Cy examined each old part minutely. He even used a caliper to make sure a used part still had the proper fit. When all else failed, Nat and Cy piled on the Harley and went off to scour the used parts places.

While Cy tinkered, Nat studied the state motor vehicle bluebook, sitting on the back step. The section on motorcycles had a lot of good tips on riding as well as the legal regulations and restrictions he had to know to get his license amended. When he knew it by heart, he went around to the registry and passed the exam.

Cy whistled through his teeth as he worked. At other times he scowled, whispered dirty words under his breath, and snarled when Nat asked, "What's the matter?" Occasionally his face brightened with pleasure as he held a part in the palm of his hand and said, "Isn't that beautiful? Now there's a beautiful thing!"

Nat watched and listened. On the days Cy whistled or scowled or swore, he studied the BMW repair manual. The other days he listened to the stories and the eulogies to various mechanical devices and knew that he was closer to where his brother lived.

When all the parts were laid out and cleaned and repaired or replaced, Cy was ready to reassemble the machine, and he said, "I wish I had a torque wrench."

Nat went around to the nearest cycle shop where the uncle of a friend of his worked, but when he walked into the old garage, the mess gave him a shock. Not every mechanic was neat as a pin, not by a long shot. While he waited for his friend's uncle to stop working, he saw a sign on the green metal tool cabinet beside his bench. It read, THESE TOOLS ARE MY LIFE — DON'T ASK TO BORROW THEM. Nat left without saying a word.

The report didn't surprise Cy. "You know that kid had one," he said. "I saw it on his workbench."

Nat borrowed the old sedan and went out to the kid's house and talked him into lending it for a few days. The kid was crazy to do it, but he did, and Nat felt embarrassed to take advantage of him.

On a two-wheeled machine, Cy said, balance is everything. One side should be the mirror duplicate of the other side. As he put the bike back together, he applied the torque wrench to certain bolts. The wrench was built with a measuring device on it, and when Cy tightened a nut, the device measured the exact tightness. Then he turned the same nut on the other side to the same precise point.

"This is what makes a difference in a race," Cy said.

"Have you raced?"

"I've been in the pits. I spent most of my time on racing bikes."

"On Harleys?"

"Two-fifties. I just about couldn't stand it at first, the way they get ripped apart. In nine months they're junk. But tuning and timing and balance, and the split-second guess. The guy comes in and says something's wrong and he tells you what he feels or hears or the way it's actin', and you've got to go right to it and fix it and have him back on the track. I thought it'd blow my mind, but —." Cy sat back and looked at Nat. "I was good at it. It's sort of educated intuition, you know what I mean?"

"A lot of good athletes have it," Nat said.

"It's what makes a good one really good," Cy said.

Part by part Cy went back across the rows on the towel, bottom row first, then next to bottom, working from right to left in reverse order. He scratched out each number as he used the part sitting beside it until the bike was reassembled. It looked to Nat just as it had before all the work, and he wondered if it would function any better.

"Well, we'll see," Cy said. "If it doesn't, this has been a hell of a waste of time."

With the machine on its stand, Cy stood to the left side and inserted the plunger key. He checked the green light for neutral, primed the carburetor bowls with gas, cracked the throttle, flicked out the starter lever with the toe of his right boot, and stomped down hard on it. Nothing happened. He stomped down again, turning the throttle in the right handlegrip. The motor scratched, then caught, roaring. Cy grinned at Nat as he listened to the sound. A minute later he rode down the alley and out of sight. Nat waited, thinking about the noise of the engine and wondering if he would ever learn to detect one meaningful sound from another. Then Cyrus appeared at the top of the alley and bounced toward him over the rough brick pavement.

"It feels all right," he said. "What do you think?"

"Well, it sounds all right. It's noisier than yours, but that clicking noise is gone."

Cy nodded. His eyes flashed. "You ready to give it a try?"

Nat laughed. "Yeh. I guess so."

And Cy laughed. "Go to it."

"Okay."

"It's all yours."

"What are you going to do?"

"Ride alongside you."

Well, then, Nat thought, here goes.

⚝8⚝
Feeling Something

If you can walk and chew gum at the same time, you can ride a motorcycle.

— Anonymous

It wasn't as if he had never been on a bike before. He had, but this one was heavier than any he'd ever tried. "Rock it," Cy said, and Nat rocked the machine forward on its center stand. The front wheel hit the pavement, the stand scraping the bricks, and the bike rolled. Leaning into the handlebars, he pushed it around until it headed toward the alley.

God, the bike was a monster, a real mother monster! Now he had to roll it down the alley into Orient Square, which was a wide-open area with six streets radiating from it like spokes. The traffic milled, crossed, made right-angle turns. Delivery trucks of all sizes bullied their way through. You never knew what was going to happen. Boston drivers were known to be crazy on their good days. On bad days, in spells of hot weather or rain of hurricane force, they were maniacal. The bricks were greasy from decades of use and dropped oil. Nat fervently wished that his first quarter mile did not go that way.

He fastened his helmet and watched Cy rock his silver one down on his head, lean down to open the gas petcock on his Harley, and glance over his controls. He throttled, listening, and then grinned at Nat.

"Ready?" Nat nodded. "Got the tach in mind?" Nat licked his lips and went over it. "Controls memorized?" He nodded again. "Okay. First off, we've got that witches' brew in the square to get through. I'll go first. I won't do anything if there isn't room for you to follow. Okay?"

Nat nodded.

"This'll be ten-fifteen minutes." Then Cy rolled down the alley.

Nat watched him go, head-first. The brakes — right foot on the rear pedal first, then squeeze the right-hand lever. God, he hoped they'd hold. He licked his lips, wiped them on the sleeve of his jacket, squeezed the clutch, toed the gear down into first, and turned the throttle. He was in motion, head-first down the alley and then he felt the traction, the compression in first. The brakes worked, and sweating with relief he came to a stop beside Cy.

"Put it in neutral when you stop. Don't sit there with your clutch in. Follow me."

Cy pulled out into Orient Square, but having Cy in front of him didn't help. Nat had to traverse the mess on his own. Cy turned right from the alley and went straight ahead, taking the shortest way out. A van cut in between them, and a VW full of girls swerved around him, the horn blasting. He clutched in panic. Damn them! They cut in front of him and turned up a one-way street the wrong way. They honked hilariously, backing out right toward him. He swerved around them, feeling the bike's tires slipping. He rolled the throttle away, squeezed the clutch, and toed the gear back into first. Slowing, the bike righted itself. He pulled up beside Cy as he waited at a light.

"Stupid broads," Cy yelled.

Nat felt the sweat trickle from his helmet. The light changed, and Cy moved out, yelling, "Watch the pavement — this street is full of shit."

It was true. The traffic was less, but now he had to keep an eye out for bumps, holes, rocks, slippery litter. They were enough to raise his tension even higher. In front of him Cy was practically zigzagging to avoid the obstacles.

By the time he reached the second light, Nat had gone to 4,000 rpms, shifted into third and down again. The coordination was coming.

"Switch on your headlight," Cy told him.

The next stretch of road they had to themselves but for one oncoming car straddling the center line. Did the driver see him or not? He gave a little to the right. The car continued down the middle. They're crazy, Nat thought, and they're fools, too.

Farther on, the road swung around a rocky hill with a park and it was empty. He let the machine out, getting up to 4,200 rpms, shifting into fourth. The wind lapped the edges of his glasses and dried his eyes. A horizontal cramp grew at the base of his neck. And then suddenly he forgot the discomforts, the tension, the strangeness. The machine moved smoothly over the winding road. The black surface flew toward him, under him, past him on both sides. He swept under the great trees lining the road, through their dense cool shadows into sunlight. Going around the last bend, he leaned into the turn, deeper and deeper, and the machine responded to his command. When he pulled up at the traffic light beside Cy and touched his toes for balance and waited for the signal to change, he laughed to himself. Now he had an idea what Cyrus lived for. He began to understand.

Cy grinned and squinted at him.

"All right!" Nat yelled. "Outtasight!"

He was nervous again when they hit Orient Square on their return. He had to come in on one spokelike street, go partway across the square, and go off on the one-way street behind the deli. He geared down, took it in first, and realized as he went up the side street that it hadn't been anything like as bad as it was earlier. He pulled up beside Cy in the space behind the deli and heaved a deep breath.

Cy eased his helmet off, squinted at him, grinning. "You look good on that machine. You may hold up."

"What's that supposed to mean? I did all right. I made it, didn't I?"

"Tomorrow we'll try a little shakedown cruise, and we'll find out for sure."

⦾ 9 ⦾
Shaking It
Down a Little

Be good to it, and it'll be good to you.

— Anonymous biker

That night Nat didn't sleep. He lay staring up at the long sag his brother's weight made in the mattress overhead, having an attack of acute nervousness. I'm not a biker, he thought, tossing. Whatever made me think I was? I've gone bananas. And then, laughing almost aloud — but tomorrow I'm hitting the road — me and my bike.

He was certain he didn't sleep, but somehow he missed Cy's jumping down. He got up and pulled on his blue jeans and a T-shirt and tied his track-type shoes.

"You look terrible," Aunt Rose said. She sat on the sofa in her robe and rollers watching the *Today Show.* "And this is your big day." She looked at him carefully. "Go take a shower. Wash your hair. I'll fix you a big breakfast. You'll feel better."

He wandered into the bathroom and peeled his T-shirt. What was the matter with him? He looked gray and drawn. I'm scared, he thought, dammit. Not scared he couldn't ride it but scared he'd fall off the damn thing in front of Cyrus.

He pricked the yolk of his fried egg, worrying and listening to Cyrus's Harley come down the alley and idle in the back. Aunt Rose looked out the kitchen window and said, "That leather suit — he isn't like the same person." Cy's boots cracked against the stairs. Then he was in the kitchen, and suddenly the room felt very small.

"Come on, man! Today we're hittin' the road!" He pulled off his gloves and removed his goggles.

In that outfit he could ride with the Angels, Nat thought, wondering if he had. There was a lot he still knew nothing about. Aloud he said, "I'm just about with it."

Aunt Rose, still in her robe, came downstairs with them and stood in the little paved yard while Nat sat on the bike and Cy loosened the U-clamps and set the handlebars for him. "This is temporary. Later on, after we've been out awhile, you'll have the feel of just where you want them."

"Did you set the carb?"

"We'll pull off somewhere and do that. The engine's got to be warm."

Aunt Rose called, "They're about to leave, Joe." Their uncle came out, flour dust to his elbows from mixing the day's pizza dough. Nat stomped down on the starter lever, and it kicked off first try. Cy started up. The little courtyard echoed with the idling motors, like racing cars waiting in the pit.

"Don't take no chances," Uncle Joe said. "Where you going, so we know where to look?"

Cy laughed. Only his teeth showed, his lips drawn back with irritation.

"We're going north up the coast, Giuseppe, but look for us

right here by seven o'clock." He kissed Rose, gave Nat the nod, and accelerated down the alley.

"Well, here goes," Nat said. He snapped up his letter jacket, set his sunglasses firmly on his nose, kissed Aunt Rose, who almost wept, shook Uncle Joe's floury hand, thought to himself, one down and three up, squeezed the clutch lever, twisted the right-hand throttle grip, and followed Cy down the alley to the street. At the red light on the corner he pulled up beside him.

"Do you know the way out of here?" Cy asked.

"Do you really want to go up the coast? That's the closest way out to the country. I'd just as soon get out of the city traffic until I get used to it."

"Lead the way," Cy replied. "The oil is pretty slick on this old brick pavement. The sooner we're off it the better. I'll be right behind you."

When the light turned green, Nat went first, accelerating carefully. Before he reached 4,000 rpms, he approached the next traffic light and had to slow down. He squeezed the front-wheel brake grip as he pressed down on the foot brake. He felt the back dragging more than the front. He must learn to exert the same amount of pressure by hand and foot. Suddenly he felt the rear tire slipping. The oil coating on the pavement kept it from taking hold. He eased the brake pedal. The traction increased, and he came to a stop at the signal. Cy pulled up next to him and gave him thumbs up. Through beard and goggles Nat couldn't read his face.

He held the bike steady, touching both feet to the street. As the light turned, he was off, Cy right behind him. Two blocks till the next light — this time he got it up to 4,000 on the tach, lifted the shift lever with his instep, and went into second.

Then the signal changed, and four green lights in a row showed ahead. Risk it, he thought and accelerated. Five thousand on the tach. He shifted into third.

Turning his head left to right, glancing into the jiggling rear-vision mirrors, scanning the pavement, listening to the motor, to the sounds of other vehicles coming and going, he found himself reacting with almost automatic reflexes. Self-preservation is a big thing, he thought, and laughed. As Cy passed him, he made a quick thumbs-up. With his left hand of course.

Cy led the way across a stretch of bad pavement. Huge cracks, potholes, whole chunks of raised concrete broke the surface. Cy threaded his way through the obstacles like a broken field runner. Side by side at the next light he yelled, "Don't they fix the streets back here? That looked like the big quake in Frisco."

"Just testing your shocks, I guess," Nat said. The light changed and he went ahead. A good feeling warmed him. He relaxed a little, losing attention for a second, then brought himself back. The sensation of close comradeship bloomed inside him. So this is what it's like, he thought, and smiled.

On each side of the street the triple-decker apartment buildings covered with asphalt siding gave way to warehouses and long, low factory buildings set back behind chain-link fencing. In turn these made way for a strip of quick-food drive-ins and gas stations and odds and ends of stores where they had to keep a sharp eye on cars and trucks turning and slowing and pulling out. Half the drivers acted as if they didn't see the motorcycles. By the time they were out in the country, Nat was wet with nervous sweat. Cy passed him and signaled him to pull off into a rest area.

As soon as he stopped, Nat was uncomfortably warm and unsnapped his jacket and took off his helmet. Cy lifted the saddle on Nat's bike and selected some tools from the bundle in the box underneath. Nat sat on the curb to watch.

"I know what accounts for the high accident rate on bikes. It's the car drivers."

Cy laughed, squatting beside the bike to adjust the carburetor. "They think you're shit. To them you aren't anything livin' that goes crunch on the street."

"Did you see that white pickup? I thought he'd take my leg off."

"Now you're talkin' like a biker." Cy wiped his tools and his hands on a rag.

"Does your jacket hike up in back?"

Cy shook his head. "That jacket lettin' the breeze in?"

"Front and rear. These snaps don't do anything over thirty."

By the time Nat had snapped up his jacket, settled his helmet, and mounted his bike, Cy had ridden off. This time he didn't wait for Nat to pull up beside him at the stop sign. When Nat turned onto the highway, his brother was already some distance ahead. It irritated him. Cy and his competence — you played it his way or you didn't play. What did he know besides bikes? Probably nothing. Now he was far ahead. Nat turned the throttle, accelerating. Water began to seep from his eyes. He hunched his shoulders forward to counteract the wind pulling at his jacket.

Going down a long hill, Cyrus increased the distance. Nat

watched him go, his brother leaning forward over the machine, his head tucked behind the windshield. There was no one, nothing else in sight on the long descending ribbon of highway, and bike and rider grew smaller and smaller until they disappeared around a curve.

Cy's gone! The aching emptiness cried out in Nat, and an instant later anger flooded him and he cursed Cyrus.

In spite of his sunglasses, water streamed from the corners of his eyes. He could feel it cold on his temples. The wind forcing between the snaps chilled him. Where his jacket rode up his back, his pants pulled down, bowing out. The wind filled that space, too. Now his insteps ached from pressing the shift lever up. He could feel every eyelet cutting the flesh.

He slowed to twenty-five miles an hour, but it didn't help much. Passing through the woods at the bottom of the hill he felt the chill of the shade. There was a four-cornered intersection ahead, and he slowed further. Cyrus was out of sight.

A gas station and café occupied one corner, and another motorcycle was pulled up beside the café window. He could warm up and maybe talk with somebody. He turned off and came to a stop next to the other bike. It was a 500 Honda, a small pack on the luggage rack. Inside he glanced around for the rider. There was only a long-haired girl at the counter, but when he sat down two or three stools away and spun toward her, he saw the helmet under the jacket next to her. It was green with MS. AMERICA across the back.

"Hi," he said. "Did you sell your other bike?"

She looked at him for a full minute and then smiled, tossing her hair back. "Finally. Did you find the right one for you?"

"I don't know if this whole scene is for me." He ordered

hot coffee with lots of milk. The woman behind the counter had chrome-yellow hair and hard eyes that hardened more as she looked at them.

"Where's your brother? Didn't he come with you?"

"He was accelerating last time I saw him. I guess he's in Maine by now."

"Some buddy."

"This is our first day out — kind of a shakedown."

"So he's helping a lot by streaking out of sight."

Nat slurped some coffee. "That's a 900 he's on. I got a 500."

The girl glared at him. "What difference does that make? He helped you buy the machine, didn't he? He knew that all along. What the hell does he think he's doing?"

"I don't know — he's really into this, you know. It's his meat."

"But that's the big thing," the girl exclaimed. "He's leading. He should bring you along, not run out on you the first chance he gets." She studied Nat. "He doesn't know sh —"

"Watch your language," the waitress said, wiping some spilled coffee.

"— know how you feel about the road. It's rough at first."

Then Nat told her how the wind blew between the snaps and up his back and the shift lever pressed the eyelets into his instep and his sunglasses didn't keep his eyes from streaming cold tears. She was incensed and exclaimed, "Damn him. He knows all about it and he didn't give you more tips! That's just what's wrong with bikers. They aren't a real fraternity."

Nat was about to reply when he heard a sudden roar outside, the door swung in, and Cyrus in his black leathers strode into the café. If he saw the girl, he ignored her, yelling at Nat, "Goddam shit! Can't you keep up? Jesus, I thought you'd racked it up!"

The girl spun off her stool and shoved Cyrus in the chest. "You're the goddam shit!" she yelled.

Cy held her off with a backhand swing. "Get off this case or you'll get hurt. Damn you, Nat —"

Nat was on his feet and shouting. "Leave her out of this or I'll kill you."

"The day you kill me I'll be a paraplegic." Cy swept the girl aside with another back-arm and grabbed Nat by the jacket.

"Get out of here," the waitress screamed, "get out before I call the cops. Get out! I've had enough of you bike riders. I'm calling the cops right now."

Nat shoved Cyrus again. The girl opened the door. In a split second the three of them were outside, and the waitress locked the door behind them.

"See what you've done?" the girl said. "And I hadn't finished my sandwich."

"Dammit," Cy said. "Dammit. I figured you were laid out somewhere. When I saw you weren't right behind me, I —"

"You shouldn't have gone way ahead like that without saying anything first," the girl said.

Both Nat and Cyrus looked at her. Cy took off his goggles and looked at her again and then laughed. "Where'd you come from?"

"Dammit. Now my helmet's in there." She knocked on the glass door and pointed to her helmet and jacket. The waitress brought them to the door, opened it wide enough to hand them through, and locked it again.

"I didn't think about you getting worried about me," Nat said.

"Yeh. That's the first thing you think of when your buddy doesn't show up." Cy took off his helmet and rubbed his matted hair, noticing her for the first time. "What's your name?"

"Gage. Where are you two headed?"

"Nowhere in particular," Nat said. "We're just out for the day to see how my bike runs before we hit the road."

"I'm just day-tripping, too. Mind if I join you?"

"That'd be great," Nat said.

Cy settled his helmet over his head, rocking it down with his hand on the crown. "It's all right with me, if you can keep up. I don't want to worry about two novices." Then he laughed, pulling his bike off the stand. Nat and Gage followed him.

A few minutes later the three motorcycles moved in single file up the next hill. Behind them the waitress unlocked the door.

At ten minutes to six Nat turned into the head of the alley and brought his bike to rest behind the deli. He was alone. After they took Gage to her place, Cy had gone to the Harley-Davidson dealer for a special oil. Bone-tired, Nat had come on home. His left instep throbbed so he half expected blood to squirt through the eyelets of his shoe each time he lifted the gear lever. And you shift a million times, he thought, pulling the heavy bike backward onto its stand, turning the wheel and locking the forks. Standing beside it for a second, he realized how automatic most of the motions had become.

When he stepped inside, his uncle was making grinders behind the counter. He looked him over darkly, not stopping or speaking.

"I'm an hour early," Nat said.

"I need help five o'clock, not six." Uncle Joe put the grinders in the pizza oven to warm. "What happen to your brother?"

"He went out to Revere to the Harley place."

His uncle didn't respond, and Nat considered how that might sound to some one who feared and hated motorcycles. He felt a wave of irritation with Uncle Joe. "I'll clean up and be right down."

Hours later Cy still had not returned. Nat built pizzas without knowing what he did. Aunt Rose came down to help with the after-movie rush, and they were silent and the customers grumbled, "This place used to be alive. What happened? Somebody die or something?" Nat couldn't think of a funny answer. They were about to close when he heard the low heavy throb of the Harley motor outside, and Cy came in.

"Why didn't you call? Dammit, we were worried." Nat leaned on the counter and glared at him. For a moment Cyrus stared him down coldly. Then he pulled off his helmet. "Okay. We're even."

))10((
Shifting
Gear

*No matter where I'm goin', I
remember where I've been.*

— Narragansett beer song

The next morning Cyrus laid out his touring gear on the
floor of the shed. In one pannier he carried personal items: a
pair of jeans, a towel and soap, toothbrush in a plastic bag —
there were advantages to growing a beard — a couple of T-
shirts, a sweater, longjohns. In the other were spare parts and
the owner's manual. A flashlight. Cy inspected everything as
he laid it out. He had a small tent, a sleeping bag, a one
burner stove and a large enamel cup. In the cup he packed a
small jar of instant coffee, another of dry milk and sugar that
he mixed together himself.

"Where do you carry your food?" Nat asked.

"I don't."

"Then what do you cook?"

"I'm not into cookin'."

"Not even breakfast?"

Cy laughed. "You're a hungry kid."

"Everybody eats."

"Figure out your own system. I get up, fix a cup of coffee while I'm packin', drink it and hit the road. That's my system. You carry what you want. The stove will go for both of us."

Nat turned away, thinking. He'd never camped out, he had never slept under the stars, and he hadn't spent any time thinking how you rustled up your eats or your shelter on the road. Now he was no longer worried that he'd fall off the machine in front of Cy. He had picked up a new worry. How was he going to get acquainted with the great outdoors without looking like a big fool?

"You got a sleepin' bag?"

"Yeh —" Nat hesitated "— but I've never used it, outside, that is."

Cy lifted his head and studied him. "Where've you been all this time? Inside?"

"You don't play baseball indoors, but I just haven't, you know, I mean —" He stopped mumbling, and Cy said, "Man, you're lucky I came back."

In the space next to Cy, Nat began to line up his own gear. Uncle Joe gave him an old stainless-steel pint measure for a cup. In it he packed tea bags and sugar cubes, a lunch-box salter and a little jar of powdered orange drink. What else he'd do, he didn't know yet. Hanging loose like Cy might become his way, too. He had longjohns, two pairs of jeans (one he'd wear), a couple of T-shirts, an old sweater, several pairs of socks, a denim windbreaker. His winter boots would hold out. A heavy riding jacket was another problem.

He and Cy toured the cycle shops for leathers, but Nat didn't want to spend the money. Even the jackets on sale cost fifty dollars, and the cheap ones had only one zippered pocket.

Cy's black leather jacket had four pockets with zippers, both a zipper and snaps on the front closing. The zippers had little chains dangling from them so you could grip them with your gloves on. The stainless steel gleamed menacingly against the black leather. Nat saw it now as just practical, not the badge of a hood, not necessarily, anyway.

In the end he decided to stick with his quilted nylon parka. It had pockets enough and would repel the rain. The only problem would be stuffing it somewhere when he didn't need it.

That saved him fifty bucks, which made him feel good. Then he blew the money on a pair of goggles, a Gerry-model pack with four horizontal zippered compartments, and a handful of triple-hook elastic tension cords.

They had to put off their departure a couple of days when the Harley place called Cyrus to fill in for a sick mechanic. Before he left, he advised Nat to pack his bike with an eye for balance and for keeping the center of gravity low where it belonged. Once it's loaded, give it a test run, he said, and check the handling. Even a few lopsided ounces will make it unwieldy and hard to control.

Nat laid the pack across the rear luggage rack and figured out a way to strap it on with the bungee cords. By hefting each item in his hand he judged the weight and tried to distribute it evenly. His toilet kit about equaled the loaded stainless steel cup. He divided his clothing — there wasn't much of it. Cy already carried the gear that went for them both.

Uncle Joe came out to take a cigarette break and watched him.

"I'll be in for the lunch rush," Nat said.

Uncle Joe asked, "You got a knife?"

"I have my pocket knife." Nat looked up at him, wondering what his uncle was thinking.

"I didn't mean no switchblade." Muttering, he went back into the deli.

Later, Nat cleaned up and put on his apron and worked behind the counter through the lunch hour. It didn't make his uncle noticeably more cheerful. During the afternoon lull he went upstairs where Aunt Rose was doing some sewing on her day off while she kept an eye on *The Edge of Night.*

Nat slumped on the sofa. "What's he down on me for? He said it was okay to go, and I'm still working in there, helping out. Right up to take-off."

"He's kind of hurt, Nat," Aunt Rose said.

"About what?"

"He loves you, Nat. He's — wild about you. You're the son he never had. He's brought you up. You're a good boy. Everybody tells him so, like he was your father. He's proud of the deli and he's taught you everything about it. You've been close, and now Cyrus comes in like a flying ridge and you're close with Cyrus. You're doing Cyrus's thing. All of a sudden he knows he's old. He's all alone now, Nat."

"But you're here, Aunt Rose. He's got you."

"That's not the same, but it helps." She glanced at him and smiled. "We had a good time, you know, the three of us, going to the games, us watching and you playing —"

Nat picked up the satin sofa pillow and punched it. If a log feels anything when an ax splits it in two, he thought, this is how it feels, like living hell.

"Don't you worry. I'll take care of Joe. You do what you want."

"What I want!" His voice was a cry. "Jesus! I don't want to

leave him. I mean — I want to go — but I don't want to leave like this. Why'd Cy show up, anyway?"

"He's your brother. A brother's a brother, Nat. You've been with us. Now you go with him. Joe'll be all right."

Miserable, he watched Aunt Rose take a few stitches in the embroidery she held close to her nose. Then he jumped up and clattered downstairs and out in back. If he had to feel miserable, he might as well feel it in motion.

He checked the bungee cords, decided his pack was secure, and stomped down on the starter. The next moment he rolled down the alley, thinking he should go out to the Harley place and tell Cyrus he wasn't going, but he knew he was. Instead he turned onto the airport road where the mid-afternoon traffic was light. He took all the turns he could find, sweeping into the deep bays of the arrival stations, accelerating up the ramps to the elevated departures and down along the empty international terminal, where he slowed and stopped and started again. He felt sluggishness, a kind of wobble in the left turn, not much, because he had been careful. The sensitivity amazed him.

The second day Cy rode his bike to work and tuned it on his lunch break. Nat took the torque wrench back to the kid. That evening they were ready to hit the road. "If I can find my jeans jacket," Nat said. "I don't know where I put it."

Cy growled, nervous and tense. "I've been coolin' here for a month now. I'm not waitin'."

"I've been waiting on you the last two days." They eyed each other warily. Nat licked his lips.

"Tomorrow," Cy said. "Tomorrow mornin' we move out."

That night Nat felt as if he lay stretched out on a narrow plank. His life lay behind him. In front of him was the road, experience as impenetrable as the darkness around him. He didn't sleep well. The morning found him dull and sluggish, the way the bike was the day before, he thought, sitting up and rubbing his head with both hands.

Rose had the coffee made and cereal and bread on the kitchen table. Cyrus only wanted the coffee and took a mug downstairs. Nat sat down with Aunt Rose, but neither of them said much. "I've gotta get going," he said and she said, "You gotta, Nat." He went down.

The two bikes, packed trimly, stood side by side behind the deli. Cy was setting his helmet. His black jacket was zipped up; he was ready. At that moment Uncle Joe came out of the deli with two white-wrapped tubes. He held them out. "A couple subs for lunch. Compliments of the management."

Cy stared at the packets, and for a second Nat thought he'd turn them down. Before he could do it, Nat smiled, stepped in, saying, "That's great, Uncle Joe. Here, I've got a place for them. I can stick them into my pack." Cy said nothing, firing his machine.

"Wait!" Aunt Rose called above the roar. She appeared with Nat's jeans jacket in her hands. "I had it all the time!" She held it up for him to see.

Across the back below the yoke a design had been painted. It showed the sun rising behind a hill. Rainbow spikes sprang like hair from the sun, which had green eyes. Out of its laughing mouth ran a road like a black tongue with a yellow line down the middle. "One of the girls at the store painted it," Aunt Rose said. "I did the embroidery." Around the tips of the sun's spikes she had stitched the words "Brothers of the Open Road."

Suddenly Nat could have wept. He put one arm around her

and the other around Uncle Joe. The three of them held each other for a long tense moment. Aunt Rose sobbed, and tears ran down Joe's cheeks. When they broke the circle, Joe took the edge of his apron to wipe them away.

Cy grinned a little, raised his gloved hand, and moved down the alley.

Stomping on the starter, Nat fired his bike on the first try. He listened to his motor, twisting the throttle over and back. He snapped up his jeans jacket, rocked his helmet well down on his head, and set his goggles, glancing from Rose to Joe. What could he say? No one of the trio could speak.

He set his boots on the foot-pegs, shifted into first, and moved toward the alley. He felt the dense magnetic field of home pulling him back, clinging to him, but the forward motion strengthened, carrying him on, breaking the barriers. As if of its own will, the bike rolled down the alley.

In an instant the deli, Uncle Joe and Aunt Rose were behind him. Ahead was a bike and a biker in black leathers and a line of green lights. He was into the road with Cyrus.

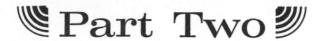

Part Two

GETTING
INTO IT

))) 11 (((
No Easy
Riding

There's more than one road.

— Gage

For the first three or four blocks Nat glanced from the street ahead to the tachometer and watched the needle moving up toward 4,000 rpms as he accelerated, falling again as he slowed for the intersections. When the next light turned red, he pulled up beside Cyrus and idled in neutral.

Cy grinned at him. "Where the hell are we goin'?"

Before Nat could reply, the light changed and Cy took off in a spurt. Nat swore to himself, but the next moment he was too engrossed in running his machine to think about Cy.

Another bike came toward him on the other side. Nat found himself noting the make, the extras, the gear. The biker raised his left hand as he passed, and Nat lifted his in reply. Inside him a kind of warmth spread out and he relaxed. Maybe there really was a brotherhood of the open road.

Up ahead Cy signaled a left turn. Where the hell was he going? Nat followed. When he caught up with him at a light, he called out, "Where are you headed, anyway?"

"How should I know?"

Again the light turned green, and Cy was off, Nat following. They crossed the Chelsea River and rode through the area which had burned to the ground a couple of years back and still bore fire scars, and passed under the great concrete substructure of the expressway. The next time they idled side by side, Cy said, "You're luggin'."

"What?"

"Luggin', and when you're not luggin', you're racin'. Watch the tach. You've got to keep the rpms right for speed and gear. Listen to it. You'll get the feel of it."

Cy sped away. The next moment Nat saw him moving up the ramp onto Interstate 93. Fear prickled over his body. A moment later he shot off the ramp and took a place between flapping Fruehauf mudguards on the trailer ahead and a great blunt-nosed truck tractor behind. Jiggling across the rearview mirror he saw KCAM in huge square letters. Jesus, he groaned, I hope they see me. If they close this gap, they pop me like a paper bag. He'd better move out.

He glanced sideways, back into the mirror, sideways again, and leaned into the left-hand lane, accelerating. The vacuum seemed to suck him toward the side of the truck. He clutched the handlebars. Then he shot ahead of the trucker and the wind hit him crossways, blowing him toward the next lane. He leaned to the right, but too much, then straightened dead ahead.

He had just pulled clear of the truckers when he saw Cyrus off on the side of the road. He eased toward the breakdown lane and pulled off and came to a stop.

"What's the matter?"

"I lost sight of you. How'd you like those big mothers?"

"I thought I'd get blown off the road or sucked into them or crushed. I really clutched."

"There's no big rush," Cy said. "Today we'll ride awhile and take a break, ride and break. We're just goin'." He laughed.

They rested for fifteen minutes or so, stretched out on the grass beyond the shoulder, before starting out again.

The traffic thinned as the interstate went north. The big trucks exited for Stoneham and Woburn. After Route 128, countryside appeared beside the asphalt. Tall pines closed on the northbound lane. Where the highway had been blasted through rock, black slate walls shone like silk in the sun. Off to the right a pond reflected sky and clouds.

It's beautiful, Nat thought. A Greyhound bus passed, giant tires humming. He stiffened and clutched. He must keep his mind from wandering.

Cy was in plain sight ahead, his right-hand light blinking like a yellow eye. Nat followed him down the exit ramp across the interchange and into an Exxon station. Half a dozen other bikers had gathered on one side of the building. Nat walked around and stretched, pressed his hands into the small of his back, and wandered over to the Coke machine. Two girls stood in the doorway, watching him. When he glanced their way, they smiled quickly, and when he moved back toward the others, they attached themselves to him, asking questions like, "Is that your bike?" and "Do you have an extra helmet?" They lounged on one foot, smiling and tossing their hair and showing their belly buttons between low-cut jeans and knit halters. When the other bikers drove off, they went with them.

"You see what a bike does for your macho?" Cy squinted at him.

"I've got to pick up a guest helmet. They weren't worried about anything but their heads."

Settling his helmet, Cy roared with laughter and kicked the sidestand out of the way.

When they set out again, the great highway was almost empty. Nat felt the wideness of it, so many lanes, so much open space on either side of him. The wind gusted across the road, hitting him sideways without warning. For an instant, he feared he would be blown off the fork, his hands ripped from the handlebars.

By mid-afternoon his back ached, his knees had cramped, and his fingers were rigid as claws around the grips. His left, clutch hand ached sharply, not to mention the back of his neck and his straining eyes. When he saw the big sign for public camping and Cy's right-hand signal winked its yellow eye, he felt an enormous surge of relief. If the bike had not had its own forward motion, it would have wobbled from side to side as he trailed his brother off the interstate.

As soon as they came out on the local road, the camping signs disappeared. On a hunch they took off to the left but found nothing inside of five miles. Turning around, they ticked off ten the other way. Still no campground.

"Dammit," Cy yelled. "We don't want to push it today."

A gas station attendant gave them directions. They got lost again on a dirt back road through the pine and maple woods, but in the end they found it, Cy cruising ahead along the campground road.

Nat trembled with relief. The day was almost over. Within minutes the ache from the small of his back through his shoulders to his forearms would slacken. Cy wheeled and came back.

"This looks pretty good," he yelled. "Find a place where we can pitch the tent, will you? I'm goin' for some finger-lickin' chicken."

"We've still got the subs," Nat called out. Cy didn't hear. With a roar he was off.

Nat rode forward over the bumpy cinder road and picked a campsite with a picnic table. He didn't really care if it was the best one. It was a place to stop. He pulled off and sat astride his bike for a minute. Then he turned it off by pulling out the key, and peeled his gloves and removed his helmet. His head felt shrunken and bony. He rubbed his hair and got off. The ground felt oddly firm under his feet as the vibrations of the road continued through him. He had to pull backward several times before he got the machine on its stand and made sure it stood squarely.

His whole body trembled slightly as he moved around. He didn't unpack anything. He made it to the bench attached to the picnic table and stretched out, wincing as each sore point in his back hit the hard wood. "Oh, God!" he groaned. In a moment sleep swept over him like a wave.

He may have slept only minutes when he twitched and fell off the bench. He stood up, and, brushing away a few pine needles with a limp hand, lay down again, thinking, now I know what it means to fall asleep.

The next moment great motorcycles were roaring through his head. He tried to stir, shake them off, but he was too slow and heavy. Another roared through his dream, another and another until the steady, uninterrupted sound rose and fell, coming closer and going away. He woke and covered his eyes with his arm, shaking his head. Then the sound came on again, almost on him. He rolled his head to the side and looked out.

Not eight feet from him stood a Harley as big as his brother's. The rider sat with his legs thrust out, black boots and black leather pants, black leather jacket, impenetrable dark goggles, a helmet of multicolored flames.

The second Nat looked at him, he turned away and gunned his engine. Nat caught sight of the back of his jacket. It carried an insignia — a winged death's head.

Nat's heart popped into his mouth, and his body tensed with a twitch. He hadn't been out a day — he hadn't gone a hundred miles — and already he had run into a Hell's Angel.

⚞ 12 ⚟

On the Side of the Angels

Mellow down easy.

— Paul Butterfield

Carefully Nat rolled his head on the bench so that he could observe the scene from under his arm. A dozen Harleys were pulled up about sixty yards away. The riders stood around, talking among themselves and surveying the campground. Slowly Nat rolled his head back to the other side and took in his own camp. His bike was maybe eight strides away and ready to go. Sixty seconds, perhaps a minute and a half, were all he needed. At the moment he made ready to move, he heard footfalls crunch in the cinder roadway and then thud softly on the pine needles. He uncovered his eyes and sat up.

Opposite him stood three bikers. One of them had ripped the sleeves off his jacket and bared his huge arms. The second was slight and carried his shoulders hunched and his hands in his pockets as if he felt a chill. The third was dressed in black leather and reflecting sunglasses that mirrored Nat's face. Nat's throat closed up suddenly. The big fellow put a foot on the bench and leaned his forearm on his thigh. The other two lounged casually with their weight on one leg.

Sitting down with his legs under the table, Nat was at a serious disadvantage and he wondered how to change his position without arousing suspicion. His throat opened, and he said, "Hi."

They looked at him silently.

Slowly Nat swung his legs out and stood up, stretching slightly and then tucking his shirt in, all the while thinking that escape to the main road was about a hundred-yard dash and he could make it, but at that moment a phalanx of giant motorcycles roared toward them.

"You travelin' with us?" the fellow with the monster arms asked.

"I'm with my brother."

"Yeh?" said the one in the mirror glasses.

Nat's scalp prickled. "Yeh," he said.

At that moment, Cy's motorcycle rounded the turn and came into view. They watched him as he pulled up, shut off the machine, swung off, backed it onto its stand and untied the chicken bucket from the luggage rack. He set it on the table and took off his helmet and goggles before he spoke.

"Hi," he acknowledged the first two, and then to the fellow in the mirror glasses he said, "Hi, Ruckus."

"Hi, Cyrus."

"Have a piece?" Cy opened the bucket.

"That's about enough for two," Ruckus said, but the fellow with his shoulders hunched against a chill looked at it longingly.

"What are you guys doin' here?"

"George got killed. Down in Florida last week."

"George?" Cyrus straightened. "George Pepperall?"

"Yeh, murder. We're going to put him to bed tomorrow."

Cy scraped his teeth over his upper lip. "Did everybody come on?"

"Everybody," Ruckus said.

Nat felt adrenalin shooting through his bloodstream. Cy and Ruckus exchanged single sentences with a long silence in between until they began to move off together. Nat watched their backs as they walked away, his brother and the three Angels. He was forgotten.

Nat took out a piece of chicken and ate it. He tried a buttered soft roll but it lumped in his mouth. Only Italians know how to make bread, he thought, and threw the rest of it into the woods. He lit the butane stove and put on a cup of water. It came to a boil, and he dropped in a tea bag. Cy hadn't come back. He ate another piece of chicken, listening to the big motorcycles leaving the grounds. Where was Cy, anyway? Maybe he should walk over to the Angels' camp and see what was going on. Instead, he sat immobilized on the bench. His fatigue had vanished in a squirt of adrenalin.

Cy didn't come back. After two hours Nat set up the tent, crawled in, and stretched out on his sleeping bag. The giant Harley-Davidsons continued to roar in and out of the campground. He felt the vibrations in the ground, and he was certain he never slept. By daylight, when his head ached and his stomach had turned to stone and his eye sockets to sandpits, he was surprised to find Cy stretched out beside him. Nat examined him for signs of abuse. Cyrus slept like a cat.

Nat tried to worm his way out without disturbing him, but Cy began to stir, opened his eyes and rubbed his beard.

"What happened to you? I didn't know where you'd gone."

"We went into town to the funeral parlor. It's George Pepperall, all right." Cy followed Nat out of the tent.

Nat tried to phrase the first of a hundred questions, but Cy went on, "They want us to ride with them today in the funeral procession. They've only got sixty-eight bikers here, and they want a formation of ten rows seven abreast."

"You go, Cy. I'd look pretty funny on a BM 500 alongside all those superpowered Harleys."

"You won't embarrass them. They want to put you in the middle."

"I'd feel —" Nat began and stopped. Cy had taken out his wiping cloth and had begun to polish his bike. The cigarette in the corner of his mouth curled smoke into his right eye, making him squint and grin devilishly.

"Shine it up, brother. You're ridin' with the Angels today."

The hand Nat held out for the cloth shook a little. Cy laughed. Nat wiped the gas tank, wishing his stomach would ease up.

Cy pulled on his leather pants. "What do you want to eat, Nat?"

"Nothing."

"No cold chicken, huh?" Cy laughed again.

"I don't want to heave in front of those guys."

Glancing at him, Cy lit the butane burner. "How about a cup of tea? That should loosen the knots and give you somethin' to go on."

"Okay, I'll try it."

Things were stirring at the other end of the campground. A few tents had been pitched, but mostly the riders had slept in bags strewn over the ground. Now they began to crawl out and wander into the woods. Most of them didn't bother to go to the outhouse.

Nat sat on the bench sipping the hot tea when the big guy with the sleeves torn off his jacket sauntered over and put his boot up on the bench.

"How'd you sleep?" he asked.

"Okay."

He looked over the table and rubbed his mouth and chin.

"We're goin' in pretty quick and get some coffee. Ruckus says to meet in front of the funeral parlor on Andover Street no later than nine-thirty. You got a watch?"

Nat nodded.

"You be there." It wasn't quite a question, or a statement, either.

"We said we'd be there," Cyrus growled. "We'll be there."

The fellow stood up and shrugged and without saying anything more turned away. He didn't help Nat's stomach any.

"Do you know where Andover Street is, Cy?"

His brother laughed. "No idea. But I know how to find it. Where sixty-eight Hell's Angels are assembled. Ask anybody — they'll know."

The tea sloshed in the stone hollow of his stomach. Nat set the mug aside. Cy pulled on his leather jacket and zippered the sleeves and the front. The neckband which closed with a sticky strip, he left open. Nat considered his jeans — they were worn and dirty enough to pass — and snapped up his denim jacket with Aunt Rose's embroidered insignia on the back. The design didn't bring out his usual feeling of amused affection. He feared it would trigger mocking anger in the wearers of the winged death's head.

"Are you going to wear your helmet, Cy?"

"I'm going to wear it into town. Ready?"

A second later Cy's bike started with a roar and then settled into its low throbbing. The BM sounded quiet, kind of ticky beside it. Nat had never noticed it so much.

At the other end of the campground the Angels were already moving out. The big guy with the huge arms was still around. The skinny, nervous kid had disappeared. As Nat and Cy rolled up, half a dozen bikers fired their machines into motion. Ruckus, an old-fashioned black motorcycle cap fastened under his chin, led the way. The next moment Nat found himself surrounded by the huge, throbbing Harley-Davidsons and the hard, sullen faces of their riders. What am I doing here? his insides cried out. How in all hell did I get into this? The next moment he told himself, Quit thinking and go. That's all there is to do, so do it.

He twisted the throttle and accelerated. A little shower of pebbles from the bike ahead pinged against his helmet and goggles. In a phalanx they swept forward into the highway. A car coming toward them swerved onto the shoulder. There was plenty of room; the driver just panicked. Nat laughed. On each side of him a Hell's Angel almost brushed his elbows. The humming machines blocked out all other noises. Oncoming cars might have been silent for all he could hear. Out in front Ruckus and Cyrus rode side by side, their left fists on their thighs, their rights closed on the throttles, talking. The skinny kid pulled up beside Nat.

" 'Brothers of the Open Road.' Hey, man, I ain't never heard a that club."

"It's a local," Nat said.

"I dig that sign."

Then they were in the dead streets of Lowell, Massachusetts, among the triple-decker frame houses with three-story wooden porches in front. People on the sidewalks stopped to stare as they roared by, more than forty of them together. They passed a line of parked police cars, blue lights flashing. What's happened? Nat wondered. There were cops at the corner holding back the traffic as they swept through the intersection. We're what's happened, Nat realized with a thrilling shock.

A bike ahead of him slipped sideways and righted. "Watch the oil on these bricks!" the rider called out. Nat felt the wheels losing traction, then catching again. His heart banged.

The phalanx roared around a corner, taking both lanes. Half a block ahead, the other twenty-five riders had assembled. Some of them sat on their bikes. Others lounged on the steps of the old turreted house which had been converted to a funeral parlor. The empty bikes were lined up rear ends to the curb.

People jammed the sidewalk. Across the street more people pressed forward to see. In the old three-story school next door, kids were practically falling out the windows, even the teachers, the janitors. Nat thought he spotted the principal peering out his office window.

"What do they think this is? A freak show?" The rider next to him spat onto the pavement.

Then Nat saw the faces strained with curiosity and fear and hatred. The thin grim lips of the cops were thinner and grimmer than he'd ever seen them. He brought his bike to a stop. His heart squeezed painfully. They hate us, he thought. Those people would like to see all of us splattered on the street. People hate bikers, and the Hell's Angels are the reason why.

He was so tense and surging with adrenalin that his toes jittered on the pavement as he balanced his machine at rest.

The word passed down to get into rows seven abreast. Another big guy in a sleeveless leather vest motioned Nat to the center, and he paddled his bike into line. Nobody wore a helmet. Nat fastened his by its strap to the luggage rack. Without its whiteness he felt less conspicuous either to the Angels or to the crowd.

Ruckus appeared on the porch of the funeral home. He moved to the edge of the top step and scanned the crowd. Standing there in his black leathers, heavy boots, the crushed visor cap and his mirror sunglasses, he looked like everybody's image of a Hell's Angel. Ruckus waited.

Next to Nat the biker leaned down and opened a hole on his muffler. The pipe was straight. Nat looked around. Everybody he could see had opened their cutouts. Now the street was filled with bikers, ten rows of them, and as they fired their machines, they came alive with a roar. Cy was three rows ahead, throttling his machine. He was indistinguishable now from the Angels.

Ruckus drew one last deep inhalation on his cigarette, snapped it aside, and moved down the steps. Behind him eight Angels appeared, carrying a great steel casket. The bikers throttled till the street thundered. They bore the box to the rear door of the long black hearse and slid it inside. After it the black-suited funeral parlor men shoved the tall baskets of flowers, crowding what space was left.

Ruckus strolled to his machine and pulled it from the stand. Glancing darkly at the crowd and the cops, he walked it into position between the hearse and the first rank of the

Angels. He swung on, pushed the electric starter, and brought on an earsplitting, unmuffled roar.

Then he raised his fist. The hearse puffed a little white exhaust and purred ahead. Ruckus brought his fist down, and seventy unmuffled Harleys ripped the air.

Sixty-nine plus one. Enclosed by Angels, Nat rode the center line. Cars pulled up on curbs to get out of the way. Spectators ready to jump and run stared from the sidewalks. Nat hardened his eyes and his face. They expect us to do anything, he thought, and he felt himself acting as if he had done and would do just about anything.

The phalanx moved through the dry, sun-speckled street in a thunderclap of deafening sound. They crossed intersections on the red light and bore down on approaching traffic. Everyone gave way. The Angels didn't give, they took, and Nat felt the cold pleasure of it.

They swung under a stone arch into the deep green cemetery. The trees and grass absorbed some of the sound. It took on a different tone, deeper, sadder somehow, less defiant. The crowd was here, too, standing at a respectful, fearful distance among the gravestones.

They came to a stop, and Ruckus raised his fist again. When he brought it down, the engines suddenly ceased. The silence was a physical void.

The eight Angels carried the casket to the open grave. Soft, dark earth rose in a mound on one side. A minister, a young gaunt man with staring eyes, appeared from somewhere to stand beside the pit. He held an open prayer book. His voice murmured, rising and falling, as the casket was lowered beneath the surface of the earth. When the casket settled on the bottom, he lifted his arms in blessing.

Then Ruckus stepped up to the grave, crushed his cap between his fists, and dropped it on the casket. The burly guy pulled a ring from his finger and tossed it after the cap. Others came forward, their heads down, to send their mementos into the open grave. Nat saw a knife go, and a set of brass knuckles, a scattering of flowers. The flower baskets were banked around the grave, and the minister cried out a final prayer. The funeral was over.

Slowly the Angels moved back to their machines, one by one firing and throttling their unmuffled motors. Ruckus and Cy spoke together beside the sea of bikes. Nat waited for what came next, reading the banners on the baskets of flowers — "We'll never forget you — Bakersfield Boys," and "George 'Pepperoni' Pepperall," and, simply, "Regrets — Hell's Angels of Rochester."

Behind him the great Harleys roared and settled into low thrumming. The hearse departed; the minister followed in an old Dodge like Uncle Joe's. The Angels rode away, not in formation now, but in knots of six or eight. None of them went alone. In a few minutes only Nat and Cyrus were left. The grave diggers, shoveling earth onto the casket, eyed them suspiciously.

"Let's split," Cy said.

In a moment they wheeled through the arch, past a few lingerers. At the first red light, Cy said, "We've got to put miles between us and this town. They don't want to see another biker for a year."

Nat nodded. "I'm with you." Cy roared ahead.

The campground was empty. Nat sat for a minute astride his bike and surveyed the area. The trash barrels overflowed where the Angels had gathered, but that was the only sign of their recent occupation. Sunlight dappled the brown-needled earth and brought up the odor of pine to his nose.

"Come on, shake it," Cy said. "I want to get as far away as possible." He began to pull the tent pegs from the soft ground.

Nat tied his sleeping bag to the luggage rack.

"Are they as bad as everybody believes, Cy? They were okay today. I mean they look rough —"

Cy squinted at him. "Some of them are just bikers."

"How come you know Ruckus so well?"

Cy hesitated, his hands stopped in mid-roll on the little tent. Nat held his breath waiting.

At that moment a long blue cruiser, blue top light spinning, turned into the campground and pulled up beside the table. Officers stepped out of each side, unsnapping their holsters.

"Hi." Nat watched them, his heart thudding. They circled the table, examining what gear remained. Cyrus continued to stuff the tent into its bag.

"You guys want something?"

"These your bikes?"

"That's right."

"You got proof of ownership?"

Cyrus opened the left pannier on his cycle and pulled out the papers, squinting at them. While one read the documents, the other leaned against the table and kept them under surveillance. Cy gave one sardonic laugh while he worked.

"How come they left you behind?"

"We aren't traveling with the Angels," Nat said.

"I saw you in the funeral lineup."

"We were just filling in because they asked us to."

The officer laughed. "Yeh? You the one from California?"

"I am," Cyrus said. "He's from Boston."

"Boston, huh?" the officer said. "Got a brother on the force there."

In that second Nat read the officer's name pin. "Are you John Flanagan's brother?"

The officer brightened. "You know my brother, Johnny?"

"His beat Orient Square?"

"That's my brother, Johnny." He turned to his buddy. "They're all right."

"Sorry about this," the other man said. "We've had trouble with bikies. You know how it is."

"We know how it is," Cyrus said.

The two men got in the cruiser and drove away, the dome light off. Cy held out his hand to Nat. "Knowin' the right people always helps."

"You knew Ruckus." Nat laughed.

"It's good to know some on both sides."

They were still laughing as they fastened their chin straps and started their machines. Cy throttled out a few Angelic roars as he led the way toward the highway again.

☰ 13 ☲
Blessing the Bikes

There's nothing and nobody to hold you back.

— Harley-Davidson folder

The day was beautiful, dry and sunny, the air cool, chilling where it leaked through Nat's jacket and hit his chest. His throttle hand ached a little. He had to think about relaxing it. His instep didn't bother him anymore. It was getting used to lifting the shift lever thousands of times, and the boots helped. He'd try several riding positions to rest his back and arms.

The road ahead was empty. He raced after Cyrus down a hill and then up, rounding a curve. He liked curves. The long, easy ones he just leaned into, and the bike followed. The short, tight corners required advance judgment. The old Harley would take practically anything because it was built low and heavy, with great balance. On his BM Nat had to clear those extended cylinders. If he leaned too far, they scraped the road and shot sparks. "Observe road conditions ahead automatically," the license book advised. And it was coming to him. The skill was coming.

"The Motorcycle Operator has a view of the complete road-way," the bluebook said. It was true, too. Nat rose over the hill, accelerating. The road flew under him, and he saw it go without looking down. He observed more than 180° from side to side. Tall white pines, clumps of grass in the sandy soil, the ragged planes of black slate blasted apart to make the highway. Fresh scents rose on the morning moisture — smells new to him — country smells.

He accelerated, the tach moving upward. He'd never pushed it so far before. He hadn't been confident that he had the control. Now — now — where was Cy, anyway? There he was, reappearing ahead. Nat rolled the throttle farther. Over seventy. The wind hit him in the chest, caught under his helmet, forcing his head back. But he was catching up. On the next turn he felt himself holding the bike at its edge, finding that line where the tires held, gravity and centrifugal force in tension. Then he and Cy glided side by side, slowing to forty.

"How's it feel?" Cy yelled.

Nat grinned and laughed. "Pretty good."

"You look good."

Nat felt even better. He knew he was doing all right — he could feel it — but having Cy recognize it gave him a sensation of solidness, his inside visible outside.

"Where to?" Cy yelled.

"After you."

"Great back roads, no traffic, nice corners. This west? Okay?"

Nat laughed. "Suits me." It was a great way to decide.

A pickup with some kids in the back passed. The kids waved. They rode on side by side, their left hands resting on their thighs, until the road widened, the traffic thickened. They had to stop at an intersection with a light.

"I'm ready for a break," Nat said. He nodded toward the Howard Johnson's across the way. Then he saw the cluster of bikes drawn up around a lamppost. The Angels again? On second glance, no, they were a miscellaneous collection, not all Harleys. On the green they crossed over and pulled up beside the others.

A guy sitting on a stack of tires watched them suspiciously. Maybe these guys were a sign, Nat thought, resting his bike on the sidestand and removing his helmet. He was looking over one machine with shining chromed forks extended about six feet to a little wheel no bigger than a tricycle's when he heard a girl say, "I didn't know you were coming."

There stood Gage in her yellow buckskins, goggles up on her green Ms. America helmet. She lapped an oversized ice cream cone.

"Where'd you come from?" he exclaimed.

And Cy said, "More important, where're you goin'?"

"What do you mean? Aren't you going, too?"

"Been plannin' it for weeks," Cy said. "What is it?"

"Why, the blessing of the bikes, of course. We're all going." She called to the guy on the tires. "Are you going to get something? Because we've got to get moving."

A thickset biker in a battered brown jacket came toward them, looking at his giant wristwatch. "Gotta get goin'." He sized up the brothers without speaking to them. Another tossed his paper cup aside and put on his starred and striped helmet.

"You goin' to the blessin'?"

"Wouldn't miss it," Cy said, kind of flipping his beard as he rubbed it.

The six bikes were all different: Gage's red Honda 500, two older bikes with extended chromed forks, a beaten-up Yamaha 250, an old BSA, and a brand-new Honda 1000 with a shaft drive. They drew up at the Ho Jo's exit, the brown-jacketed guy in the lead. He turned north.

Cy and Nat fell in with them, and the eight bikes traveled in a wedge, like geese. The two-lane road rose and fell as they swept along, curving through the hills. It took them through woods and farms and along old stone walls lined with giant sugar maples.

At a five points, some other bikers with Connecticut plates came up from the west and fell in behind them. Three guys riding bare-chested on ridiculously chopped machines came in from the east. After that every crossroad brought more riders onto the road.

Nat relaxed in the sunny day and felt the warmth of companionship flood through him. Bikers were really great, automatic buddies, he thought. And then he saw the black and purple bus pulled off the road. Behind it a dozen guys stood around their bikes, the backs of their jackets covered with the Heaven's Devils insignia. They were setting up flagpoles on their bikes and adjusting great black and purple banners bearing their sign.

His body prickled. He saw the scene ahead: a great fully chromed cross made of an outsized extended fork and handlebars. Somebody in black leathers and reflector shades was acting like a priest — and God knows what was going on as the spring rites of bikers. He wasn't going to get sucked into this. He accelerated until he came up opposite Cy and Gage and yelled, "I want to talk to you. I'm going off at the next rest area."

Cy nodded. A few minutes later they pulled off into a black-topped parking place.

Nat got off his machine and let it rest against the sidestand. He walked around it to Cy. "Check me out of this blessing bit."

Cy pushed up his goggles and studied him. "What's got you so uptight all of a sudden?"

"That." Nat jerked his head toward the road. The squadron of Heaven's Devils swept along the curve, black and purple banners flying. "The funeral yesterday was enough for me, at least for this week. I'm checking out."

"You don't have to join their club," Cy said, and Gage exclaimed, "But the blessing's really straight."

"Have you been to it?"

"No, but I know it is," Gage said.

"Who told you? That big guy with the wristwatch? I wouldn't trust him as far as I can throw my bike."

"But it's legitimate, Nat, I know it is."

"It was a legitimate funeral, too. I mean they didn't bury him alive."

At that moment a black BMW hooked with a matching black BMW sidecar pulled up beside them. The rider took off his helmet and rubbed his graying hair. In the sidecar his wife threw back her fur lap robe and stretched. "Thank God, not too much farther to the shrine," she said to Gage.

"Is that where you're going?"

"We go every year. Wouldn't miss it." She stepped out stretching.

Gage glanced at Nat. "Now are you satisfied? Even rich BMW riders go." Cy squinted at him sideways.

Nat said nothing, stomped the starter, and got on his bike.

From there on the highway thickened with bikes. When they turned onto 4A toward Enfield, the state police were out directing traffic. Along the edge of Lake Mascoma, bikes and cars moved slowly toward the shrine.

More state troopers waved them toward the open meadow beside the lake, where people had pitched camp in vans and tents. Hundreds of bikes were parked or moving among them. Farther on, to the right, a great field climbed the hill. There another thousand bikes milled. The trooper waved them to that side, and they turned into the parking lot in front of an old square stone building. More bikes than anyone had ever seen together whined and coughed in the lanes. How many were there, Nat wondered — three thousand, four, five, maybe?

"Oh, damn! We missed the mass," Gage exclaimed. "Lines are forming."

"Well, let's get in one," Cy said. "That's what we came for, isn't it?"

Lines going where? Nat wondered. He was going to find out before he followed. But he didn't have a chance. Someone warned him to stay in place and not foul everything up. Cy went first, then Gage. They had taken off their helmets. Nat left his on. So had others.

The line moved swiftly, the machines under power, up a wide asphalt walk toward the white-robed figures on the hill, then veered to the right in a deep hairpin and returned in a double line toward the priests. Suddenly the line stalled. Nat looked around. The Heaven's Devils, banners flapping, were right in front of the two priests. Beside him and behind him came the Social Riders of Boston, black men in yellow windbreakers. The line moved forward again. A young priest — and he was a real priest — lifted his silver sprinkler and shook holy water on Cy, on Gage, then Nat. He felt the drops like rain on his face. The line stalled again, then moved, swinging around the opposite hairpin, back to the center walk and down to the meadow at the foot of the hill.

"So that's it," Nat said and laughed. Cy grinned. "What did you expect?"

"Well, bikers can be a little raunchy," Gage said. "Look."

An extended fork machine zoomed past with a rider who had a gold nose ring attached by a gold chain to his single gold earring. A three-wheeler with a fiberglass cab shaped and painted like a death's-head took its place in line.

"Look now. Here comes the nursing home contingent," Cy said.

They watched a line of white Harley 1200s ridden by gray-haired men in red jackets. Gray-haired ladies in matching red jackets rode behind them and great American flags fluttered above the machines.

"I guess it takes all kinds," Nat said. And Gage added, "And that's a blessing in itself."

≋14≋
Talking

Together in song and prayer we ask the blessing
of the Almighty on the knights of the road.

— A La Salette priest

In the parking areas the riders gathered by twos, by clubs, by groups. A Moto-Guzzi club was all couples in their thirties, while the people on the big matching Harleys were even older. The Huns, the Heaven's Devils, kept to themselves, and no one challenged their right to do so. Nat strolled by the BMW club, listening for a few minutes as one rider talked about touring Africa. "We only hit one bad stretch crossing the Sahara," he heard him say. Nat's brain prickled. There were worlds out there, worlds and worlds. One door opened onto the next.

"I'm hungry," Gage said. "I wish we had a picnic. All I've got is apples."

Nat snapped his fingers. "Two subs coming up."

"You guys are incredible! You've got just about everything."

"Just about — nuthin'!"

They rode their bikes to the edge of the parking lot where

they could watch the line of bikes still moving uphill toward the priests. Beyond the asphalt they found the grass thick and long. Nat took the white-wrapped subs from his pack, wondering what they would be like by this time. While he cut a third off each one for Gage, she unzipped the side of her buckskin pants, which weren't pants but more like cowboy chaps, and took them off. Her jeans were underneath.

"Where'd you get those?" Cy was greatly admiring. "Or did you make them up?"

"I used to wear this outfit showing horses. Lots of horse people have these."

They settled on the grass; Cy stretched out on one elbow, Gage cross-legged, and Nat with one knee pulled up. They ate in silence, watching the bikes.

"You know," she said finally, "I really feel different. Kind of blessed."

Nat watched a couple on an antique Indian motorcycle move up the hill. "It makes a bike seem more respectable. I wish Uncle Joe could have been here. It'd make him feel a lot better about the whole deal."

Cy said, "Maybe we can send the scene to Giuseppe. There was a guy between the lines with a Polaroid, shootin' as fast as he could pull the paper out. Maybe he snapped us goin' past."

Gage brought the apples from her bike pack. "Don't you guys have any parents? Who's this Giuseppe?"

"We aren't Italian," Nat said, "but he's our folks."

"Yours. I don't have any." Cy laughed.

"How come? You are brothers, aren't you? You have to have parents."

"The old man was regular army," Cy said. "Got into a

helicopter accident in Nam. How old were you, Nat? You even remember him?"

Nat shook his head.

"Then Ma died from drug shock. She wasn't very sick, but she couldn't take some hotshot prescription. We were already livin' with Giuseppe and Rose. Rose was her sister. I was eleven, goin' on twenty," Cy said. "And after that, it was trouble, man, big trouble." He laughed.

Nat studied one apple, turning it in his hand. After a minute he said, "I was six going on forty. I was no trouble at all."

Gage laughed. "You guys are so different. I mean, you just aren't alike."

Suddenly again Nat felt the doors inside him opening. He had been straight long enough. His glance fell on his machine, sitting aslant below, the great American freedom machine. Girls were yours for the price of a guest helmet, the roads were free. It could make him his own man.

It was mid-afternoon before the long lines of bikers stopped climbing the hill toward the weary priests. The two fathers had filled and refilled their sprinklers from the old gallon wine jugs of holy water waiting at their feet. The burly biker with the wristwatch strolled over to Gage and asked if she was ready to head back. Gage said she was and turned to Nat and Cy. "Where are you two going?"

"Just hittin' the road," Cy said.

"You really hang loose." She laughed, pulling on her buckskin chaps and zipping them down. "What about your straight man?"

"I'm sticking with him for now," Nat said, only half joking.

"I could meet you someplace next weekend, if I knew where you'd be."

"There's motocross Saturday and Sunday in Maine — outside of Rumney," Nat said. "The guy I bought my bike from will be racing."

Cy looked up with interest, and Gage exclaimed, "That's great! I'll meet you at twelve noon in the Rumney town square."

"If it has one," Cy said.

"Oh, it has one. This is New England, not your mucked-up California."

Nat laughed. She was right. There were things every New England town had, like a town square and a white church with an icicle steeple. You could count on them.

She got on her bike, pressed the electric starter, and shifted into first. "See you in Rumney." She flicked her warm red-brown hair over her shoulder, glancing back. "Wherever that is."

Cy watched her go and murmured, "Well now, that's a foxy lady, I must say." He looked at Nat, squinted menacingly, and laughed.

"What's that supposed to mean?" Nat felt anger rising. He squinted back and laughed.

"She's too old for you," Cy said.

"Maybe she likes younger guys."

"You're real touchy, aren't you?"

"Yeh."

"Me, too."

Tense and angry, Nat thought, this is stupid. Gets us nowhere. He watched Gage disappear down the road.

15

Into
Weather

Ride to live and live to ride.

— Biker's slogan

In front of the old stone building one priest, in his black shirt and pants now, had put on a purple ribbon to bless one last latecomer. The biker stood head and shoulders above the middle-aged father, who read briefly from his prayer book and squirted a few drops of holy water from a squeeze bottle onto the machine.

The blessing was over. The riders headed out, almost all of them riding double, girls on behind. There weren't more than a handful riding their own bikes like Gage. Nat missed her. She brought a lot of class with her.

Cy found the Polaroid photographer and came back with two black-and-white pictures. One showed Cyrus with Gage's profile and the front end of her bike. In the other Nat was passing the young priest just as he shook his sprinkler. Nat tucked them inside his jacket for the time when he could send them to Rose and Joe.

They crossed Lake Mascoma on the old Quaker bridge and

headed north, staying clear of the superhighways. On the narrow back roads frost and snow and heavy snowplows had scarred the blacktop. Dodging the ruts, the wind in his face, kept Nat alert. The frequent curves which had given him pleasure in the morning now added to his fatigue. It was time to quit, but Cyrus pressed on.

Finally they took a break. "I like this country," Cy said, walking around and stretching. "These so-called mountains are gettin' bigger."

"It's getting colder, too," Nat said. He pulled his parka from his pack and changed.

"Toughen up, city kid." Cy grinned, squinting, and took off.

Nat took his time. Follow — follow — that's what I'm doing. Damn Cyrus, he thought as he stomped the kick start.

They were into the White Mountains before Cy was ready to stop. The campground — Cy chose it — was for hikers and climbers. A few were camped in the next site. They sat around their fire, someone playing a guitar and singing folk songs. Nat felt different from them. Suddenly he saw himself as a motorcyclist, a man on a machine.

A couple of the climbers came over and offered to share their fire. Nat and Cy joined them and listened to the talk about climbing. They had ropes and axes and special heavy spikes they called pitons and $100 boots.

Afterward, back in their own camp, Nat said, "They've got as much sunk in their equipment as we have."

"And they think they're right next to nature." Cy laughed.

Nat hunched his shoulders against the cold. It was his second night, and he'd already forgotten his original anxieties about sleeping out. Last night he had had greater fears of the Angels. Now the newness was gone. Although the cold and the mountains and the forest pressed around him, he was too tired to think about them. He stretched out in the little tent, listening to someone blow lonesome blues on the harmonica until he faded away.

Waking the next morning in the little orange tent, Nat heard a patter on the nylon. He lay still, listening to that sound.

Cy lay on his back, smoking. When he saw Nat was awake, he said, "The shit is fallin'."

"We can just hole up here until it stops. I want to study the bike manual over again. It'll make more sense to me now."

Cy blew smoke toward the pitch of the tent. "I hate bein' cooped up. Holin' up in a little sprinkle like this is no place, man." He flicked his cigarette butt out the door, pulled on his leather pants, and crawled out.

Nat felt little bubbles of anger rising and breaking. The hell with Cyrus, he thought, and called out, "It'll stop after a while. What's the hurry? We're not going anywhere. We don't have to be in Rumney until Saturday, so what the hell?"

Suddenly the orange nylon collapsed on top of him. Cy was pulling the pegs out. Nat swore aloud and fought his way out. Before he could get his pants and jacket on, his shorts and T-shirt were damp, and his anger broke. "Damn you, Cyrus. What the hell's the hurry? Now it's coming down harder, for chrissake."

"Put your helmet on. You'll never notice." Cy scowled, packing his gear, pulling up the tension cords in swift strokes.

"You just want to go through a lot of hell, that's all. I don't have to do that to know I'm living. I get my kicks steering clear."

Cy shrugged. "Wait it out then."

Nat's anger bubbles popped more slowly. I don't want to be separated from him, his inner voice told him. At least not yet. He stopped swearing, zipped up his parka, zipping inside as much moisture as outside, and hastily packed his machine.

Cy stowed away the little stove. He wasn't even going to make instant coffee. Nat watched him squat beside his machine to check it out, a morning routine as automatic for him as going from bed to bathroom. Raindrops stood out on his thick hair, oily and matted with sweat from the helmet.

"Check your bike!" Cyrus yelled at him. "Don't be stupid. A day like this, you don't want more trouble."

The rain running under his collar, Nat checked the oil level and took a handful of wrenches to test what might have loosened from vibration. Things felt pretty tight. The cables hadn't frayed, and there were no oil leaks.

"Wipe it off!" Cy yelled.

"In this rain what for?"

"So you'll know what's happenin' today, not yesterday. And step on it."

By the time Nat had wiped the road grime from his bike, mumbling dirty words to himself, Cy had fired his machine, flicked on the headlight, and stood waiting. As soon as Nat got on, he pulled out ahead.

Nat's mood grew worse. The rain increased. It hit him sharp as needles. At thirty-five, forty mph he felt it seeping in under the rubber padding around his helmet. It shot up from the front wheel, soaking him to the knees. And his knees didn't need it. They led the way like dual prows on a boat.

It grew darker, the rain heavier. Nat rode a little behind to the left of Cy, back out of the spray. Lights were on in gas stations at an intersection. There was a café attached to a station, but Cy rode on through.

Damn him, Nat thought. He gunned his machine until he came up beside his brother and yelled. "Let's get in out of this. I could use some breakfast."

Cy shouted something and shot ahead.

Nat swore at the top of his voice and pounded the handlebar with his left fist. Punishment, that's what this whole thing was about. See how much self-inflicted pain you can take. His goggles fogged again, and he bent his head and shook them clear. When he looked up, he saw the break in the pavement. His right foot sought the brake pedal. His right hand released the throttle and closed on the brake lever. The rear wheel slid to the left. He let go, gearing down, skidding again. Then his bike shot off the blacktop and hit the mud, spewing it out on each side like the wake of a speedboat. From the corner of his eye he saw Cy flounder and sink, the muck from Nat's wake showering over him. Nat held on, dead ahead. The BM whined, spun its wheels, slowed. A second later it hit the lip of the pavement and came out of the mud hole. He turned onto the shoulder, hauled his bike onto its stand, and ran back.

Cy was standing beside his Harley, swearing himself blind. "Goddam hog, goddam hog. Quit your goddam laughing and push."

Nat grabbed the right handlebar and the back of the seat and dug in. "Didn't you see it coming? I sure didn't."

"Sure I saw it comin'. I figured I'd power through it, but the goddam bike's too heavy. You went through it like a mosquito. Did you have to pass so close?"

"I just barely saw you. It's so damn dark. I didn't see the break until I was on top of it."

They pushed the Harley through the muck and onto the pavement. Cy inspected to see if the mud had gotten into anything important. Then he revved the engine a few times. Nat paddled his machine into the road, waiting. This time they set out side by side.

A mile or so farther on they came into the outskirts of a town. The road became a street with gas stations, motels, quick-food places on either side. They slowed, the rain bouncing off the pavement, passing cars spraying them with wakes like speedboats. There was a diner set back from the street, some big bikes parked beside the entrance.

Oh, God, Nat groaned, the Angels again. And Cyrus was turning in.

≋16≋
Talking
Bikes

We are wired for dreams, running, and riding.

— Lee Gutkind

The bikes were all different. Nat saw at a closer glance a huge Harley 1200, a couple of Honda 450s, and two other smaller Japanese machines. All of them with panniers or packs or homemade boxes. Not Angel bikes.

The windows were so steamed up Nat couldn't see inside. Then his goggles fogged when he hit the warmth. It took him a few seconds to find the man who said, "Here come two more."

Empty helmets and jackets dripped from stools. Gloves lay, wet palms up, on the counter. Halfway down the diner a little knot of people watched them, and the man's voice called out, "Two coffees on my tab. A couple of road men are in serious need." The group laughed a little, welcoming them.

Cy laughed, pulling off his helmet. "Man, you'd better believe — "

"Not fit for man nor Harley," their host replied. He was an older man, as tall as Cyrus, with rough gray hair. His dark blue jumpsuit had red and white stripes on the sleeve and a star-spangled numeral one over the heart. It was unzipped, showing a red down vest underneath. A tiny white-haired woman in an identical suit stood next to him. She had a mug of coffee in one hand and a doughnut in the other. A little powdered sugar dusted her dark blue suit. They looked dry as bones.

A girl in jeans and a nylon windbreaker sat on the end of a booth bench, shaking so hard that she couldn't drink her coffee. Her boyfriend was even wetter. Nat knew him for her boyfriend because his chest was soaked but his back was dry where she had hugged him, riding.

On the other side of the booth were a mother and father with their ten-year-old son, all of them in rain suits. They must be on the big Hondas, Nat thought.

Nat's cold fingers closed stiffly around the mug, his middle finger through the cup handle. He sat down on a stool with his back to the counter and said hi to another guy about his age and just as wet.

Right away the talk turned to bikes. Nat wanted to know about the Harley 1200, obviously ridden by the numeral ones. "But can you feel the road?" he asked. "I mean, it's like a flying armchair with running boards."

"Foot rests, son, foot rests."

"Don't let him kid you," his wife said. "It's a super sofa."

The other guy his age wanted to know how long Nat had been into bikes, how long they'd been on the road, and had Nat ever read *The Bikers* or *Zen and the Art of Motorcycle Maintenance*.

"The what?" Nat asked.

"Or Thompson's *Hell's Angels?*"

Nat felt put down and said the Angels hadn't mentioned the book when he rode with them the other day. The guy almost lost his teeth for a second, and then he said, "Well, reading isn't everything — you know — but it's a dimension. Say, was Sonny Barger there?"

"Well, I don't know. We weren't exactly introduced."

The others fell to arguing heatedly the relative merits of Japanese makes. The father knew all about Soichiro Honda's life story right down to his getting a pair of pliers on his third birthday.

"They wanted me to take on Honda in '59," the older man said. "I'd been a Harley dealer for twenty-five years then. I laughed my head off. That little scooter, I said. We had seventy percent of the market. Now we've only got about ten percent, but we're selling twice — three times as many machines."

"Honda made it a life-style," the father said.

"It's good and it's bad," the older man said. "Sales are up, but so's the accident rate."

"We've got to teach kids how to ride," the father said. "I wouldn't send this son of mine out with a car or a shotgun without teaching him how to handle it. But nobody teaches bikes. You can't get a high school to dare offer riders' ed. The parents would come on like you were initiating the kids into the Devil's Disciples."

Then the conversation turned to the outlaw gangs: were they as bad as they are made out to be?

"Lee Gutkind thinks the news and the movies made the Hell's Angels," Nat said. "Brando was pretty convincing."

The older man watched Cy, who said nothing. "What do

you think?" he finally asked. "Anybody in leathers on a Harley 74, California plates, must know something."

Cy sipped his coffee and didn't offer a reply.

"What about the races at Loudon?" the young guy asked. "Is that a bad scene? Are you going up there?"

"We aren't," the mother laughed. From his seat in the booth their little boy watched all the faces.

"Sometimes there's big trouble up there," the older man said.

"Nothing's gone wrong the times we've been there." His wife brushed at the powdered sugar.

"It's a great race — the Nationals," the older man said. "It's a damn shame when it goes bad."

"Why do they get so uptight about a motorcycle race?" the young guy asked. "Riots happen — lots worse ones — at soccer games, rock concerts, you know. People have it in for bikers."

"If bikes were really straight, it wouldn't be half the fun," the girl said. She had stopped shaking, and her boyfriend said, "You feel free on a bike, and freedom is never really respectable."

"What do you mean by that?" Nat asked. "Freedom's what America's all about, isn't it? You know, 'sweet land of liberty, let freedom ring.' "

Cyrus and the young couple laughed with derision. The little boy's parents laughed, too, but sadly, and the older couple looked unhappy.

"There isn't any such thing as freedom." The father glanced at his little boy as he spoke. "I don't mean that cynically. Freedom works out to mean freer than something else. Beyond the old limits."

"Rules, discipline, that's what makes you free," the old man said. The other man looked about to argue the point, but the old man turned to Nat. "Every morning now you're on the road, you make your quick visual check, right?" His glance was so stern and sharp that Nat murmured, "Yes, sir."

"That bike's a freedom machine as long as you look after it, take care of it, show it some respect. Then you're free to zoom over the landscape, part man, part bird, part machine."

Cyrus stopped laughing and nodded. "Nobody's got rules like the outlaw gangs. The Angels are a real tight society."

Everyone studied Cy again as if he had secret knowledge, and the girl said, "But nobody thinks of that when they see us go by, you know. The people with cars and houses — they think we aren't obeying any rules at all."

"That's what I meant by freedom not being respectable," her boyfriend said, and everybody agreed. They talked on and ate bacon and eggs and white-bread toast soggy with butter until the rain let up. The man who ran the diner gave them a sponge and rags to wipe their saddles and machines dry. After shaking hands and giving thumbs-up the older couple mounted their super sofa, turned on the power, and rode out. The Honda family followed, the little boy in his helmet lettered PETER riding loose behind his father. The two-stroke Suzuki sounded extra noisy as the young couple got under way. Then Cyrus's machine wroomed and purred.

"Tell me the names of those books again," Nat asked the young guy as they got ready. He listed them, adding, "What about Loudon? Do you think you'll go to the races?"

"I don't know. We haven't talked about it."

"I wish you knew. I want to go but I don't want to go alone."

"Yeh, I know what you mean," Nat said. "My brother's masterminding this trip, and maybe he's thinking about it, but so far he hasn't let on. He's got gear oil for blood, so he might do it."

Nat grinned, stamping down on the starter and mounting. He rocked his helmet down on his head, settled his goggles, and made thumbs-up. Then he pulled out, gunning it too much. A moment later he gave a small inaudible cry: oh Jesus! I'm going down!

))) 17)))
Laying
It Down

There's no such thing as a free ride.

— American proverb

Afterward when he went over it, he knew what had happened. It happened like this. He pulled into the curb break
leading out of the diner's parking lot and looked right. The
opposite lane was clear. Nothing coming. A bakery truck was
pulled up on the far curb, but it was stationary. He sat on his
bike, leaning on his right leg, his left foot poised over the
shift lever. He glanced left. A pickup camper with a trail bike
on the front bumper was coming toward him. There was
room, if he powered it. He could get in front of the camper
and catch up with Cy. He shifted into first, gunned into the
lane, swinging in a wide arc almost to the center stripe. Then
he looked up.

A giant station wagon had swung out around the bakery
truck. It was coming right at him. The driver's face was
shockingly clear. She was looking to her right, at the truck.
She didn't see Nat at all.

Without thinking Nat cut sharply to his right, shortening

his arc. He hit the hand brake. The front wheel grabbed. The back of the bike slid out from under him. The next instant his right leg slid over the pavement. His right hip struck the road. His helmet bounced. He heard, felt the plastic crack against the street. His head, his vision fogged. Then out of the blur he heard the whine of his engine racing. The throttle was jammed! Driven by the rear wheel, the bike was spinning on the pavement. Somehow he got to his feet. The front end spun toward him. He reached for the plunger key, yanked it out. The motor coughed and died, and the bike came to rest against his boot.

Brakes were screaming. Next to his right shoulder he saw the trail bike with the camper behind it and the driver's mouth open and twisted.

Nat grabbed one handlebar, gripped the frame under the seat, bent down, thrust his thigh under the gas tank and heaved the bike up. At that moment the college guy from the diner jumped off the curb. "You okay?"

Nat nodded.

"Jeese, that was close."

In the backed-up traffic, horns honked angrily. They wheeled the bike off the pavement.

"You sure you're okay?"

"I'm okay."

"That station wagon just missed — the rear wheel was half an inch from your head."

"Yeh?" Nat swallowed. "Got to check the bike. Hope the bike's okay." They wheeled it into the parking lot and pulled it back on its center stand. His pack was still on straight, and that made him feel good. He had really secured it, and the slide couldn't have been too bad. He walked around his bike.

Nothing had broken that he could see. But everything on the right side that stuck out had been scraped — the throttle grip, the cylinder-head cover. The muffler bore a long streak of tar.

"You've got a little asphalt on the back of your parka," the college guy said, "on the right shoulder. Kind of a hash mark, I guess."

"Yeh, a road sign." Nat tried to laugh, but it came out squeaky and shaky. He put his foot on the kick starter and stomped with all he had. Nothing happened. He smelled gas. It was flooded. He kicked it again. This time it caught.

The other guy stood back. "You're sure you're okay?"

"I'm okay."

The bakery truck waited across the street, the driver watching. Nat gave him a wave. The woman in the station wagon never had seen him. Then he throttled, listening to the motor.

"Thanks a hell of a lot," he said to the college guy. "Maybe we'll see you at Loudon."

"Right."

Nat pulled into the curb break again, and glanced both directions twice before he pulled out. This time he switched on his headlight. A short distance down the street he began to shake. His body shuddered in waves. He tightened on the handlegrips and fixed his eyes on the road. Then he began to feel the bruises, his right shoulder, his butt, his tailbone, the road burn down his right leg. The pulsing in his head beat against the helmet padding. With every throb the pain grew.

Ahead he saw Cy pulled off reading the map. He stopped beside him, a little behind. Cy didn't turn fully around to look at him.

It was much later, when he woke in the middle of the night crying out, his body iced with sweat, that Cy finally said,

"You'd better get some crash bars to protect those cylinders."

Nat stopped his teeth from chattering. "Protect the cylinders! You've got your priorities mixed up."

Cy laughed. "You've done about all you can to protect yourself. You're goin' to be in some tight spots from time to time. You bend one of those cylinders, and that'll mean some big bucks."

Nat wiped his face with his T-shirt. "That big station wagon missed my head by half an inch."

"It'll give you nightmares for a while."

"Like the rest of my life. How many times have you gone down, Cy?"

"When you're bikin', that's not one of the things you count." Cy laughed again. "But I've had a little practice."

〰18〰
Crossing
the Notch

*Some guys ride to win, and some
guys ride to find themselves.*

— The Duke

The next morning Cy spread out the map across the handlebars and put his finger on a spot on the Kankamaugus Highway east of Lincoln. "We're here," he said. "In this campground. How about goin' this way?" It was more a statement than a question. He drew his finger east, then north.

Nat walked around, checking out the various parts of his body. He was stiff from the damp night, from tension, from the slide on the pavement. His shoulder and butt ached. In certain positions pains shot outward from the places where he had landed. Worst, his right leg burned like fire where it had slid across the asphalt. He had lost some skin, but he had only one small rip in his jeans.

After he'd checked himself out, he gave his bike the quick morning once-over. Gas level, oil, air pressure in the tires, all were okay. Was there any fraying on the control cables, any loose or broken spokes? He moved around the bike from the right handlegrip back to the right handlegrip, trying a couple of bolts to see if they had vibrated loose, while Cy checked the Harley drive chain for grease and proper tension. Since the BM had no chain, Nat fired his machine and let it idle in neutral. He was ready. It gave him some satisfaction to show Cy that he was waiting for him. Cy chose the route, but this morning Nat led the way.

Although the day was overcast, the cloud level seemed to lift as the wide black road wound higher into the mountains. The air was cold striking Nat's face, the pine forest thick on the right. Railroad tracks appeared where the terrain leveled off, opening out. A pond sparkled beside the road. Next to the tracks there was a little depot that had been turned into a restaurant. Nat, still leading, swung off and went inside without waiting for Cy. He had already ordered a stack of blueberry pancakes when Cy came in. The whole thing made him feel much, much better.

Some guys in their twenties ran the place, and did the cooking accompanied by a continuous tape of Joni Mitchell. Their eyes brightened at Nat's account of the morning ride.

"Have you been over Jefferson Notch?" the cook asked. "That'd be a great road on a bike."

"How do we get there?" Cy asked.

"Stay on 302 to Bretton Woods and go right toward Mount Washington. Watch for a little dirt road on your left. You'll see the sign."

"Okay," Cy said, and Nat burned a little. His brother never asked him what he wanted to do, not that it mattered. The Jefferson Notch road was all right with him, but he wanted to be consulted.

After pancakes and coffee and warming up in front of the depot fireplace, they went on. The clouds lifted and broke just as they came into Bretton Woods. Sunshine lit the snow-covered shoulders of Mount Washington and an immense white hotel. "That thing's mother big!" Cy exclaimed. "Bigger than the White House," Nat said. They turned right, leaving the inn behind, and the clouds closed again on the mountains. The road rose, and there on the left was a sign for the Jefferson Notch road. A couple of orange-painted barriers blocked the way — CLOSED FOR REPAIRS. Cy didn't even stop. He exploded past Nat, swerved around the orange sawhorse, and disappeared beyond the first bend. Nat swore, pounded his gas tank with his fist, shifted into first, and followed. What else was there to do?

The road was paved for a few hundred yards. Then Nat shot off the asphalt onto sandy gravel. His tires bit in, slowing him down. He geared back to third. The road was wet, he noticed. It had rained here yesterday, maybe during the night. The forest pushed right to the edges of the road. Below, on his left, a stream splashed and roared and tumbled over great wet rocks.

Nat came out of a bend to see that Cy had come to a stop. He sat astride his machine, studying the little wooden bridge ahead of him. Nat geared down, braked, stopped beside Cy. He felt his adrenalin squirt against his scalp. Half the bridge wasn't there.

The crosswise planking on the bridge was cracked and splintered. Most of it had been ripped off and thrown in a pile beside the road. The downstream guardrail was gone. Four heavy timbers bridging the stream still looked sturdy.

"I think it's closed for repairs," Cy said, laughing and rubbing his bearded chin.

"We got to go back," Nat said, but Cy didn't hear him.

Suddenly he shifted into gear and was in motion. He headed the Harley dead on toward the great cross-timber that had held the guardrail. For a minute he balanced on the beam like a tightrope artist. The bridge trembled and rumbled, but the bike didn't waver. A moment later Cy pulled up on the other side, whooping and shaking his fist above his head and yelling, "Don't accelerate! Get your speed before you hit the bridge!"

Evel Knievel, Nat thought, and swallowed. He glanced down at the boulders in the streambed below, and quickly looked away. He was supposed to do that? Oh Jesus! Then his anger boiled up again. The hell he would. He hadn't been on his goddam machine for six years. He would just walk it across.

He pulled out the starter key and got off. The only clear track for the bike was across the big outside beam. If he was careful, he could walk the next beam and guide it across. Tilting the bike toward himself, he pushed it onto the timber. It was heavy and inert, and he could feel the tenuous traction of the tire's edge on the wet wood. He looked down between the timbers just once. The streambed was rocky, the water roaring and frothing. He pushed the bike, stepped over a broken board, felt for that point of balance between the bike, the forward motion, his body. Then he found it, letting the bike lean into him and he leaned his weight against it. Picking his footing, pushing slowly and steadily, he made it to the other side.

"That's the hard way," Cy said.

"That's my way," Nat muttered. He got on his bike and set off ahead. This is the end, I'm cutting out, he thought.

The road narrowed to one lane. The forest pressed thicker and closer. The clouds seemed to be dropping lower, growing dark and ominous. Nat's bike skittered in the wet sand and gravel. The little road curved and bent backward and forward in figure S after figure S, climbing all the time. It began to snow.

Cy pulled up beside him, laughing and raising his fist in salute. "Back to nature!" he yelled, gunning past.

For a moment Nat tensed angrily. Then, as he watched Cy splash through the rut ahead, he knew he didn't want to go back. He felt the strength of the bike beneath him, its response to the throttle. Just let it hold up, he thought. Big wet flakes sizzled on the front pipes.

Now patches of snow lay in among the trees. Where the road passed along the north slope, old drifts melted and puddled in the ruts. Nat hit one, splashing up to his knees, the ice water soaking through his jeans into his boots. Great heavy flakes continued to fall. One was enough to shutter half his goggles. He smeared them away with the sleeve of his parka. Then another hit and another. He had to stop and push his goggles up on his helmet.

Cy glanced back, laughing. He thinks this is great, Nat thought. The next moment they rounded a curve and came to a stop. The road was choked with snow.

The snow was old and crusty, granulated on the surface from the melting away underneath. Cy whooped and followed his rut right into it, the machine wallowing as it pushed through the drift. Cy put out his feet and waddled it along, leaving a track like an old sea turtle on her way across the sand to lay her eggs. He honked his horn, and the sound disappeared in the trees pale green with new leaves.

Nat accelerated along his rut. The BM's protruding cylinders scraped through the crust. He horsed the throttle and paddled with his feet. The snow shoveled over his boots and up his legs inside his jeans. He shook it out. The great flakes plopped on his cheeks, melted instantly, and ran off in icy dribbles. When Cy looked back, grinning and hollering, his beard was crusted with snow. He looked like Harley-Davidson's idea of Santa Claus.

Suddenly they came over a rise and were headed downhill. The bikes picked up speed. Nat felt the weight of the machine cutting through the snow to the road, and now the weight was good, working for him, not against him. The flakes seemed to get larger and wetter, but they were fewer and melted quickly.

Then the road was clear of snow, and they were going steadily down.

He caught sight of some trail markers, then an empty parking area for hikers. The road widened again. The curves were longer and less frequent. Warm air flowed toward Nat, moving upward. The flakes vanished.

We've crossed the notch, Nat thought. It's behind me. There was asphalt underneath him again. He rumbled across railroad tracks, swerved around orange sawhorse barriers, and came out on a broad highway.

Cy pulled abreast of Nat. He was still laughing. "Didn't know you had anything like that this side of the Rockies."

"Not your ordinary run-of-the-mill notch," Nat yelled.

They raced each other into Gorham and pulled off at an eating place called The Hobbit. A fire was going inside the dining room, where they ordered hot pastrami on bulkie rolls and double-size mugs of hot coffee.

"Where are you two comin' from?" the counterman asked, in a New Hampshire drawl.

"We just came over Jefferson Notch," Nat said. "There's still some snow left from last winter."

"Last winter!" the man exclaimed. "Why, that's from year before last!"

"I believe it," Cy said.

They laughed and hung their wet jackets on two chair backs and ate their sandwiches standing in front of the fire.

≋19≋
Traveling
by Three

Be proud of what you are: a woman —
get out there and ride!

— The Insider

The following Saturday they sat on the steps of the white clapboard church facing the Rumney town green and waited. Cy stretched out, leaning on one elbow, his boots crossed on the lowest step. Their machines stood side by side, rear ends to the curb. A police car cruised slowly past.

"That's the third time, for chrissake," Nat said. "I hope she's okay." Nat hugged his knees and felt a bruise he hadn't noticed before. The abrasions burned against his jeans, and he winced. "I just felt a new one," he said.

"You're lucky you just left skin."

"Okay, I'm lucky, but dammit, I hurt, too."

"Think of the sympathy you'll get from the woman, if she shows up."

"What's keeping her?"

Cy shrugged. "Nothing we can do about it." They had waited half an hour. The steeple clock struck twelve-thirty. Then quarter to one. One.

"I think I'll call Uncle Joe. He'll start worrying. They haven't heard anything since Enfield."

"Don't tell him you went down."

"I know that much." Nat walked around the corner to the Gulf station where there was a phone booth. He shut himself in and dialed. Minutes later, above the deli's lunch-hour noise he heard his uncle's voice, "Of course I collect. Hello, Nat? That you? You all right, Nat?"

Nat assured him they were okay, in Rumney, Maine, no trouble, bikes running great. Uncle Joe didn't ask a direct question like, "You have an accident, Nat?" so he didn't have to make up an evasive answer. Before three minutes elapsed, they hung up, and a little wave of homesickness hit Nat. He took his time going back to the church steps, forgetting his dime in the coin return. He hadn't sent his love to Aunt Rose, which gave him a twinge of regret.

"Where the hell is that woman?"

Nat shrugged. "How should I know?"

"You're the one who set this up. I knew it wouldn't work."

"Why'd you go along then?"

Cyrus sat up, rubbing his beard and squinting at Nat. The cop car passed along the far end of the square, and after it appeared one solitary cyclist in a green helmet.

"The law's guidin' her in." Cy laughed.

Nat felt a surge of energy and relief.

Coming to a stop at the curb, Gage flashed her beautiful white smile and called out, "It took longer than I figured. Sorry about that. Oh, I'm beat!" She threw herself flat on the church lawn, her helmet rolling from her hand.

"Did you run into trouble?" Nat sat down beside her.

She shook her head, her dark red-brown hair spreading out on the grass. "Just one guy in a white Continental. He kept trying to pull me over. Finally he came up beside me in the breakdown lane and leaned out the window and said, What's a nice girl like you doing on a thing like that? I told him it improved my stud image. That made him pull in his face. Some men give me a pain." She sighed and stretched. Nat felt a twinge of apprehension, misgivings.

"Are there any good lakes around here?" Cy called from the steps. "I'm for cadgin' a campsite on some water."

Gage sat up. "Water! A swim would be great."

The Gulf station attendant gave them directions to the nearest campground on a lake. Then they ransacked a jumbled general store for franks and buns and chips and a couple of six-packs, paid for it in three equal shares — Gage insisted on it down to the penny — and set off over the back roads to find the place.

Where the pavement came to an end, Nat rode across the bump, the rear shocks contracting and releasing under him. That feeling he had come to enjoy. He knew through his butt what shock absorption really meant. The road, now soft and sandy, now hard-packed dirt, continued through deep hemlock and maple woods. In the sandy stretches the wheels cut in, the bikes wallowing.

"Stick to the berm," Cy yelled. He rode along the narrow hard edge between the ruts and the ditch. A few minutes later they came out at the state park gate. The ranger assigned them to the last vacant site on the water. It had an open-face three sided Adirondack shelter looking out on a little point. They parked their bikes beside it and inspected the rocks and brown-needled earth and inhaled pine scent and listened to the clear water lap-lap-lapping like a cat drinking at the edge of its bowl. Nat felt wonderfully good.

They threw their packs and sleeping bags onto the shelter floor, and dug out old cutoffs. Nat took a careful glance toward Gage as she stripped off her leathers. He didn't want to be the kind of man that gave her a pain, but she already had her cutoff jeans underneath and she left her Yamaha T-shirt on. They raced to the water and plunged into its coolness and freshness and struck out, shrieking exuberantly, toward the middle of the lake.

Cy had a long steady relaxed stroke, and soon he was way ahead, moving across the lake. Nat swam well enough, but swimming wasn't his strong suit. His school didn't have a pool — none of the city schools did — and he had been too busy to go to the Y. He and Gage swam side by side, Gage alternating strokes and saying, "You know, you've changed since the day you came to buy my old bike."

He trod water. "How do you mean?"

"You seem a lot older, you know, in charge of yourself." She floated on her back sculling.

"I don't feel it. I'm just following Cyrus. He leads. I haven't soloed as much as you have."

"You even look older."

"Maybe I just need sleep."

"You really don't want to believe what I'm saying, do you? I'm getting cold."

They struck back toward shore. Cy's head was just a knob on the far side of the lake.

Nat dried himself off, not risking a glance at Gage, and pulled on his jeans. They were soaked with grease and road soil like a mechanic's. Gage sat down on the picnic bench and hung her long hair aside to dry.

Nat was suddenly aware that she wasn't very pretty. Her ears stuck out, her neck was too long and skinny for her body, and her nose was bony and a little crooked. But she had that dark reddish hair and beautiful not-quite-perfect teeth and a lithe skin-and-bones body.

"What are you thinking?" She glanced at him suspiciously.

"Well, I — I was just thinking I saw you for the first time, sort of. You know what I mean."

"And I'm not really pretty, right?" Her glance turned a little sad.

"Well, maybe not piece by piece, but put all together the effect is terrific." He felt himself redden, and laughed.

She looked at him steadily, which deepened the red, and put her hand over his. "You're great, Nat," she said.

"You just don't know me very well. If you did, maybe I'd give you a pain."

She brushed her hair in long strokes, the damp strands loosening. "I know a good man when I see one."

At that moment Cy rose from the water, his hair and beard dripping, his chest bare, and threw his towel around his neck. "Where the hell are the hot dogs?"

"Never thought of them," Nat said.

"We were talking." Gage gathered up her brush and towel and walked off toward the rest rooms.

Suddenly Cy threw his towel around Nat's neck and pulled his face toward him. "You tryin' to make time?"

Nat stiffened. "We were just talking, like she said."

"Yeh?"

"Yeh."

Cy released one end of the towel, and Nat straightened up. A wave of uneasiness passed through him. He wondered if their traveling by three was going to work.

That night they spread their sleeping bags on the floor of the lean-to, smeared Gage's bug spray on their faces, and settled into sleep.

For a long time, Nat lay on his back listening to the cat tongue-laps of the water and the occasional cheeps and cries in the woods. Something was being eaten out there. A lop-sided, past-full moon rose late and illuminated the woods like high noon and turned the water's surface to pounded pewter. As he watched, a line of dense clouds rose on the far side of the lake, crossed the sky and obscured the moon. Suddenly the night was the darkest he had ever seen.

Then it rained. Pine scent rose from the damp needles like a mist. Drops pattered dully on the shingle roof.

So this was the Maine woods, he thought. He had lived one state away all his life, and he had never spent the night in them. Here he was and practically out in the open, too. He burrowed into his sleeping bag, suddenly aware of the warmth and the pleasant closeness of his two companions.

⚆ 20 ⚆
Tuning
for Tookie

Motocross racing is the biggest
motorized sport to hit these shores ever.

— Motorcycle Weekly

The next thing he knew Gage was sitting at the picnic table tinkering with the one-burner stove, and the sun shone directly into the shelter. Nat pulled on his pants inside his bag and got up. Cy had covered his head.

"Build us a fire," Gage whispered. "It's damp."

Nat stared into the blackened fireplace. He had never built a fire.

"Oh, you city kids," Gage said. "You all ought to be sent to Outward Bound."

"The wood's wet. I know that much."

"Peel some slivers with your knife. They'll be dry inside. It didn't rain that much. Pine cones make good starters. Put them on top of that egg carton."

"I can light that stove. You build the fire."

"No, we don't. I'll learn this, and you learn that." She laughed and tossed back her long hair.

Nat followed her directions, scraped aside the soggy remains of old fires, laid the cardboard carton on the bottom, and heaped it with pine cones and slivers of wood. On top, at Gage's direction, he laid two reasonably dry middle-sized sticks parallel to each other and crossed them with half a dozen more. "Leave some air space," Gage said. "We can feed it once it catches."

The first match set the carton alight, then the cones and slivers and, after a few minutes, the upper branches.

"You learn fast, you city kids." Gage threw him her lovely smile. She stuck the tines of a fork into a slice of bread and handed it to him. "Want a piece of toast?"

Nat sat on the end of the picnic bench and held the bread over the flame. It was smoked more than toasted, but they smeared it with butter and jam and divided it. By this time Gage had figured out the stove and made some tea.

"I love to cook out. Want an egg?"

"We don't have a frying pan."

"Oh, you guys. What have you been doing, anyway? I'll boil a couple."

Girls, Nat thought, a girl like Gage, anyway, made a distinct contribution.

"Cy doesn't go much for cooking."

Gage glanced toward the inert heap in the lean-to. "That brother of yours — I can't figure him out. Where's he coming from, anyway?"

"I'd like to know myself. This is the first time we've ever been together. He's a biker, that much is certain. If he went down, he'd feel worse about leaving paint on the road than skin."

Gage tilted up her chin and laughed. She made Nat feel wonderfully witty.

A moment later Cy sat up and threw back his bag and glared darkly at them. "What the hell's goin' on here?"

They watched warily as he pulled on his leather pants and jumped off the lean-to platform. His eyelids were swollen with sleep. Rubbing his hairy chest set the small gold medallion swinging. He made instant coffee with the boiled-egg water and glared suspiciously at the two of them. He guzzled the coffee without speaking and sauntered off to the shore. A few seconds later he came flying back, waving his arms around his head and cursing the air. "Damn little biters. Let's get out of here!"

"Break camp just for a few black flies?" Gage cried. Nat felt one under his eyelid, another up his nose. He grabbed the Off and sprayed the air.

"Throw some wet wood on the fire," Gage yelled. "That'll fix them."

The heavy smoke rolled up. They huddled beside it, their eyes weeping, smearing Off on their exposed skin.

Cy swore again. "Where'd they come from all of a sudden? What are the bloomin' biters doin' in a nice place like this?"

"God's just telling us there ain't no paradise," Gage said.

"I found that out my first day in California. He doesn't have to repeat the message. Let's get over to the track. The exhaust'll kill 'em over there."

The routine morning visual check was the quickest yet. Within minutes, Gage leading, they hit the highway back to Rumney. None of them knew where the track was. They could ask at the Gulf station, but just as the highway turned into a town street, a pickup with two motocross bikes in back passed them going the other way. Cy made a U-turn in the road. As they headed in the other direction, the pickup disappeared down a side road. They followed through the woods bumping from blacktop to gravel to sandy ruts.

Nat geared down and bounced across a couple of acres of parking field, most of it still empty. Vans and pickups and trailer rigs clustered near the pits. Beyond tall pines, unseen motors growled and whined in practice runs.

Cy pushed his goggles up onto his helmet. "Where is this kid?" His eyes gleamed with excitement.

"Maybe he's not here yet. Wait a minute." Nat bounded over a couple of ruts, looked again at a lone figure slumped in the rear door of a van. Yes, it was Tookie Hillman, all right. Nat waved the others to follow.

Tookie had recognized his old bike and stood up. He stuck his fingers into his back pockets and shuffled toward them, grinning a little, mumbling, "Gee, great."

"I'm Gage." She held out her hand.

"Gee, great."

"Where's the bright, shiny Yamaha?" Cy asked.

Tookie humped a shoulder toward the van.

"Did your dad drive you up?" Nat asked.

Tookie shook his head. "No way. This guy — bought it from — his van."

"Where the hell is he?" Cy pulled his machine up beside the van and locked it. "Aren't you going to race?"

"— Got another racer — amateur class — you know. I'm just —" his voice wandered away.

"So he just trundled you up here, huh? And now he's out with the rider who can do him some good." Cy read the sign on the van, ROGENCAMP'S CYCLE RAMA, COMPETITION BIKES OUR SPECIALTY. The trademarks of Yamaha, Bultaco, Penton, Maico — all the motocross bikes — were scattered across the multicolored side panel. Tookie's bike was inside, secured to the floor, and the van's walls were lined with shelves of tools and parts.

"Okay, okay," Cy murmured. "Let's get that bike out here and see what shape it's in. Get into your stuff. You got pants and boots and —"

"Yeh," Tookie said. "But —"

Cy snapped, "Are you goin' to ride or aren't you?"

"Well — yeh — I wanna ride but — you know — the bike — it could freeze on me."

"It's not goin' to freeze on you. What's a tuner for, kid?" Cy laughed. "Get your stuff on."

Tookie's foot missed the rear of the van in his hurry. They got the bike out and Cy rode it around the open field. Then he ran it onto a mechanic's rack and began to tinker, helping himself to tools and a couple of carburetor parts in the van. Tookie squatted beside him and watched.

"It's getting hot," Gage said, stripping off her leathers. The parking acres began to fill up. More racers arrived. The puddles from last night's rain drained, and the ruts hardened. Nat and Gage inspected the track, the looping, rolling, packed-dirt raceway cleared in the woods. A few riders took their bikes over it. It looked dry enough, except for the sand trap on the far side. They watched one rider flying into the first turn, his bike climbing the soft bank, stalling, and dropping. Then they saw Tookie wheel his machine into the starting place with Cy beside him, talking.

"Don't give it everything you've got," they heard Cy say. "Just enough to show me how you ride."

Tookie was dressed in padded yellow leather motocross pants, knee-high plastic boots with seven buckles, a loose yellow jersey pulled over shoulder pads, gloves, goggles, and a visored helmet. Nose protection hung around his neck. He pulled up to the starting line, throttled wide open, hit the clutch, and shot forward. A moment later he was in midair off the jump and down to the ground just before the first turn. Cy ran to the end of the oval to see him corner, and followed him to the sand trap, where he was lost to view until he came out again just before the far turn. He came up the final hill, crossed the finish line, and popped a wheelie before he came to a stop. Tookie was laughing. He loves it, Nat thought.

"Forget the wheelies," Cy said. "Traction is the name of the game. Stay in the groove. This dirt is loose and it's going to get looser every lap. Get your weight a little farther forward when you stand — keep that front end down, down, down. Make it bite. You ever try your handlebars turned down farther — not much? Lean with your bike in the turn. Your body's up toward ninety degrees and the bike's about forty-five — see what I mean? Yeh, I know some guys do it that way, but don't. Stick your left foot out a little more and lean toward it."

They wheeled the bike back to the van and adjusted the handlebars. Tookie sat on the seat and tried them, stood up and tried them again. He grinned. "Yeh — great — lot better."

"Okay — okay." Cy nodded.

Tookie was in the first novice class 125 cc heat. There wasn't long to wait. Gage ran off to the snack van and brought back Cokes all around. Rogencamp and his amateur racer came back, and Rogencamp was not particularly friendly. He made a list of the parts Cy had taken and put them on Tookie's bill. Cy toasted him with his Coke and said, "You may be happy to know this kid some day."

Rogencamp locked up his van.

They walked toward the entrance to the track, Tookie pushing his bike and Cy talking. "It'll be just about the same as it was when you went over it earlier. Your corners'll be tighter if you lean like I told you, so don't flinch — just hold it tight. Keep both those wheels down on the start and get them down fast after the jump." Tookie listened and nodded.

The pack of racers roared, waiting to cross the track to the starting line. Tookie fired his machine and moved to a place among them.

"Do you think he can make it?" Nat asked.

"I know he can," Cy said.

The racers moved forward, invading the track, and taking up their positions at the starting line. Nat and Cy and Gage crossed quickly to the oval inside the track.

"How do you know?" Nat asked, but his voice was lost in the noise. The racers began to throttle their machines. Two officials, one with a clipboard, went down the line checking the riders. The flagman stood back. When the men had finished and stood out of the way, he lifted his green flag. The racers throttled their engines, raised their left hands above the clutch levers. The flag came down. Twenty left hands hit the levers, and the bikes sprang forward.

Tookie was maybe eighth coming off the line, but he rose on the pegs in the jump and made an almost two-wheel landing. "That's the way!" Cy yelled. In the first turn he held to the groove, leaning at almost the same angle as his bike. By this time he had passed three others and took a fourth going into the sand pit. "Okay, just hold," Cy yelled, although no one could hear him.

His second lap was even better, but Number 97 passed him after the second turn. Coming out of it Tookie was ahead but he took the back corner too wide and climbed the soft bank, his bike screaming, the tire sweeping. "Get down! Get down!" Nat yelled. Ninety-seven moved into third and then second. As they came out of the final lap, Tookie caught the edge of the sand bank but gunned it just enough, shot up the last hill, and crossed the finish line, just barely fourth.

Cy grinned and slapped Nat on the back.

"How'd you know he'd make it?" Gage screamed.

"He's scared, but he's not afraid — you know what I mean?"

"Well, I'm both," Gage screamed, watching a stretcher carried across the oval toward the ambulances and first-aid van. "Anybody in his right mind would be."

"Nobody in his right mind is here," Cy said.

≡ 21 ≡
Tookie's
Race

Ride to win? Well, I sure don't ride to lose.

— Motocross racer

They waited near the announcer's stand until they heard Tookie Hillman given credit for fourth. He had qualified for the finals. Cyrus went off to find him while Nat and Gage stood at the fence and watched. The earsplitting noise continued. The drivers waiting on the entrance ramp throttled; an equal number at the starting line throttled; while a third group raced over the dusty track, bikes whining and screaming and roaring, wheels biting the heavy sand, driving through the mud hole in the sand trap, climbing the banks and accelerating uphill.

At the start of one heat black flags went out on the first corner. So many drivers had gone down that they started again. No one was hurt. On another lap red flags flapped as flagmen signaled the racers to take a corner wide to avoid a downed bike in the track. Men with stretchers waited at every turn. It was an exceptional heat that didn't see somebody carried at a fast stride to the ambulances and first-aid station.

Gage put her hands over her ears and rested her forehead on Nat's chest. Stirred and wondering, he patted her back.

"I thought rodeos were rough. Bucking horses always scare me. They can kill an old-time rider, but this — this — I can't take this."

Her hair smelled warm in the sun, and Nat felt wonderfully protective as he stroked it.

Gage straightened. "I can hear your heart pounding. You're scared, too. Or are you excited?"

"Well, both," he said, thinking of her pressure against him. "Kind of stirred."

"I'm just scared."

They weren't talking about the same thing, Nat thought.

When all the qualifying heats in each division were run, the loudspeakers blared, announcing a forty-five minute break, then the finals. Suddenly the noise was shut off as if a giant switch had been thrown. Gage exhaled like a balloon. They went in search of Cy and Tookie, who were back at the van working on the bike. Rogencamp was there. He had opened up his van and made suggestions. Nat bought a candy bar and another Coke for Tookie and a couple of hot dogs each for the others. They perched on the seats of their bikes and ate and talked.

"Ninety-seven is the one to look out for in your class," Rogencamp said. "He's good, but he's erratic. He gets thrown off course sometimes."

Cy listened intently and asked questions about 97. Tookie tensed when the call for the first race echoed through the trees. Leaving Rogencamp, the three of them walked with Tookie toward the entrance ramp. Nat wheeled his bike.

"Breathe deep," Cy said. "Keep the old oxygen moving. Shake your arms like a swimmer."

Tookie inhaled and shivered first one arm, then the other.

"Stay loose to the last minute. Do like I told you — get the feel of the bike."

Waiting at the edge of his group, Tookie stood on the pegs, throttling and moving back and forth to get his balance. After a few minutes he gave Cy a big grin, and Cy gave the clenched fist salute.

The first race got off, whining and screaming. The second rank of racers crossed to the starting position. Tookie moved up.

At that moment four men with a stretcher between them ran across the track to the first-aid van. A rider was limp on the stretcher, unconscious, his legs curiously lifeless in the heavy buckled boots.

Tookie clamped his teeth shut and looked away. Cy and Nat swore under the shrieking noise. Why did they have to carry him right in front of the waiting racers?

"For God's sake, back out now!" Gage cried out. "Nobody's making you."

"Shut up," Cy snarled. "I hope he remembers what I told him."

A second later Tookie swept forward with the others across the empty track to the starting position. Between laps Nat and Cy and Gage ran through the dirt to the center oval and found places along the fence opposite the lineup. Tookie was fifth from the left in the front row.

"He's got a good spot," Cy yelled, adding something that was drowned in the oncoming sound, the throttling, whining, shrieking, accelerating decibels of fifteen 125s fighting for speed in a foot of sand. The score of riders before them throttled incessantly as they waited in swirls of white exhaust.

"I can't stand it," Gage said. "My ears have stopped up." She pressed her palms to her ears, trying to pop the drums. "It's madness! They're crazy! Why do they do it? They're nuts!"

They are nuts, Nat thought as he watched.

Tookie put on his mouth and nose protection. The shoulder pads stuck out at angles under his jersey, which had come out over his kidney belt.

The flagman waved the yellow flag for the beginning of the last lap. Tookie looked their way, and they shook their fists, grinning. A few minutes later the flagman waved the first winners across the line with the black-and-white flag. The whining, shrieking noise of the race subsided, and the rhoom-rhoom of the waiting throttles increased. An official checked them out, numbers, bikes, safety gear. The track was clear. The throttling increased. The first signal was given. The riders raised their left hands above the clutch levers. The flag came down. The bikes leaped out, rear tires biting into the dirt.

Tookie leaned forward, keeping both wheels in contact. In a second he was out in front ankle to ankle with 97. Together they sped up the rising track to the jump. The earth gave way beneath them, and all four wheels spun as they flew into the air, glided and hung there, fell to the earth again. Ninety-seven leaned farther forward and brought his front wheel down at almost the same instant as the rear wheel. Tookie did more of a wheelie and fell behind. Still, he was on the inside going into the turn. The sand was deep, churned up now.

Ninety-seven flew outward up the bank. Tookie moved forward, flinching away as 97 came down across his path.

"Don't do that!" Cy yelled into the whining and shrieking and throttling. "Hold steady. Let him worry."

Tookie headed down into the sand trap, disappeared behind the hillock for a split second, then came dead toward them, upward, the front wheel sweeping and twisting as the rear wheel bit in.

"Hold it steady!" Nat shouted. "Grip it! Grip it!" No one could hear him. They ran across the center field to the downhill side of the jump. The red accident flags were out.

"Oh, God! Oh no!" Gage cried.

But Tookie and 97 came up out of the far turn wheel and wheel. The red flags waved them toward the inside. Tookie gave way and 97 moved ahead.

"Dammit!" Cyrus swore, and Gage said, "He should have held no matter what." She turned to Nat in surprise and asked, "What's gone wrong with me? I shouldn't feel like this."

"It's the race," Nat shouted, laughing. "It's the race!" He took her hand, and they ran back across the field to the sand pit. They were just in time to see Tookie come out of the turn, a little behind now, and they shouted and gave him clenched fists, not knowing if he saw them before he disappeared between the banks of sand. The red flags were furled now. The fallen rider had dragged his bike off the course.

They couldn't see the far turn of the track. It was lower than the rest, darkened by the tall red pines. The curve was sharper, not quite hairpin but close to it, the dirt and sand banks higher. Their view was cut off by the starting position. From the deep curve the track rose to the jump. Tookie and

97 came out of it. Tookie back in position inside 97's rear wheel, just ahead of the wake of sand he kicked up.

"Good boy!" Cy yelled.

Tookie came out of the jump with nearly a two-wheel landing. "That's the way!" they shouted, no one, not even themselves, hearing.

His left leg extended, his foot bouncing over the track, Tookie leaned into the turn. "That's it! That's it!" Cy pounded Nat's shoulder. "He's loosenin' up. That kid's got it now!" Laughing, they ran to the sand pit and signaled raised fists as he came out of the turn. They raced back to the jump again. Another lap and the flagman at the finish line waved the yellow flag. The last time around.

Tookie fell behind at the jump, not getting his front wheel down fast enough, made up for it at the first turn, and was a little ahead going into the sand trap. Coming out, 97 was in the clear.

"Go! Go! Go!" they screamed. The riders disappeared into the final turn, and they ran to the finish line. Ninety-seven came in sight biting the soft dirt of the bank. Tookie was into it, too, but lower, where the surface was harder. He straightened, then turned slightly to the outside — 97 flinched away into the soft bank. Tookie spurted forward, up the incline, and the checkered flag signaled a figure eight as he went over the line. He had won! Tookie stood up on the pegs, sailed into the jump, sat back, and came down in a great triumphant wheelie.

Nat and Gage sprang into the air and threw their arms around each other. Cy stood back, grinning and lighting a cigarette.

When the gate opened, they ran across the track and hurried around to the riders' exit just as Tookie was coming off the track. They ran out and Nat took his bike while Cy helped him off. Gage unbuckled his helmet and his face protection. Behind it his mouth and nose were clean, below his sunken, dirt-ringed eyes. He was grinning and screaming in a high thin voice, "I won! I won!"

"You did! You did!" Gage cried. "You were great! Oh, we've all gone bananas!"

≋22≋
Face-off

A bike is no place to thrash out your problems.

— Bill Atwood

Nat pulled up at the exit to the parking field, touched his toes to the ground, and turned to look back. At that moment he saw a guy, a high school kid in jeans like himself, standing about twenty feet away watching him and considering. He looks like me, Nat thought. A second later it burst on him that he, Nat, must look to that kid like the photo on the cover of Lee Gutkind's book — a guy in denims, astride a BMW, looking back over his left shoulder. He looked like a biker. Cy and Gage were coming up; he throttled, shifted, the rear wheel bit the dirt. He *was* a biker! And he laughed and felt wonderfully good.

They left Tookie behind with Rogencamp and headed back over the same roads they had used that morning toward the camp on the lake. Gage wanted to cook. Cy said to hell with cooking, and she said to hell with him. They stopped at a store and she bought some hamburg and baking potatoes. Cy growled and bought a six-pack of beer and muttered that

women were always trying to change things, which made
Gage mad. She said men always wanted everything their way
and had temper tantrums when they didn't win. Nat built a
fire and Gage put the potatoes behind it against the stone fireplace.

They took a swim, but Gage and Cy just bobbed and
argued while Nat swam. When they waded back to shore,
they were exchanging insults.

"What's eating you, Cy?" Nat exclaimed. "Your boy won.
You should feel good."

"I hate that goddam sport," Cy said. "They take a beautiful
machine and make junk out of it in a couple months. A good
bike'll cost maybe fifteen hundred, and in nine months you
couldn't sell me a bolt off it."

"Well, it's not your bike."

"I got feelin's, man. It makes me mad."

Nat went off with his towel and razor to find the bath-
house, where he stood under the shower until his quarter ran
out and the hot water shut off. His hair was clean. Rubbing
it, he felt it slip under the towel. All the dirt and sweat ac-
cumulated under his helmet were gone, and his head felt
light. He watched the last swirl of dirty water go down the
drain, and he felt good, fresh all over. He wished he had
clean clothes. It was a shame to lose this great feeling by put-
ting on his dirty shirt and pants. They were stiff with road
grime, but he pulled them on. Still toweling his hair, he
walked through the pines. Their scent seemed stronger and
the brown needles were silent and slippery under his bare
feet. It had grown dark, and cook fires set shadows leaping in
the campsites he passed. He smelled beef searing over flame,
and then he saw their table through the trees.

Gage sat on the bench facing him, and Cyrus sat next to her. His left arm was around her, and his right hand rested on her bare thigh. Nat watched his lips move while Gage lifted her head to throw back her hair, looking into Cy's face and glancing down where she stirred the earth with her toes.

Watching them, Nat shriveled and froze. Cy was hustling Gage. Well, he was older, experienced, a man of the road. Then Cy's hand moved on her thigh and Gage drew away. For a second Nat didn't see what he saw. Then he swore and sprinted through the trees and shoved Cy away from Gage and pushed the wet towel in his face. Cy jumped up, shoving him, and Nat fell.

"What the hell is the matter with you?" Cy yelled.

"You son of a bitch!" Nat shrieked. "Keep your hands off her!"

Before Nat could scramble to his feet, Cy pushed him off balance again. "You just want to do it yourself."

His tone mocked, seared him, and Nat came at Cy again. Cy was on him in a flash, pinning him to the earth. A sharp rock gouged his back. Suddenly inside him a dam broke, and all the anger and resentment and hurt he had felt against Cy overflowed. The instant he felt Cy relax and mutter "What the hell?," he moved and pinned him to the brown pine-needle mat. Before he could get his knee into his chest, Cy had used the slope of the ground toward the lake to roll him over. In a second they were on their feet, facing each other and breathing hard. Now Gage jumped between them and gave them both a shove.

"I'm not going with either one of you, so get it together."

"That's ridiculous," Cy said. "You'll like it in my tent."

"I like to sleep out under the stars — alone."

"Maybe you'll change your mind," Cy said.

"Maybe she won't."

"When I'm traveling with two guys, I know better than to go with either one. The hamburger's burning." She turned to the fire, leaving Nat and Cy to look at each other.

"We're goin' to have to do something about that," Cy said and laughed.

"Well, I don't know. If there isn't a winner, there isn't a loser, either."

"I like to win a little better than that," Cy squinted at him.

"I don't go much for losing myself," Nat said. He gave his brother another shove, a light playful one this time. "You're standing on my towel."

"One of these nights," Cy muttered, "it's goin' to rain."

⟨23⟩
Really
into Bikes

The road is life.

— Sal Paradise

The next morning they packed up and took off for the Maine coast. They wanted to find a road winding within sight of the sea with the smell of salt and a sea breeze stinging them alert and curves both tight and easy reminding them they were on two wheels. They were in high good humor. The three bikes purred.

"You guys are great!" Gage cried out, riding between them on an empty stretch of road.

"You're quite the woman yourself." Cy laughed, and Nat said, "Brothers and sisters of the open road." Laughing, they stood up on the pegs three abreast.

They rode over the great turnpike and picked up Route 1 going north. It went along the coast much of the time, but it was choked with traffic and beachfront towns and pizza parlors. They were all right, Nat said; it was the other places that spoiled the shore.

"Where the hell is this celebrated rocky coast of Maine?"

Cy asked as they pulled up for a rest break at Freeport. After Brunswick the road grew more scenic but more wearing. Late in the day they found a meadow sweeping down to the sea. A farmer let them pitch the tent there.

During the night fog rolled in. When Nat went off in the morning, the tent disappeared six feet behind him. Their clothes were damp and heavy. "What's more, we're beginning to stink," Gage said. They spent most of the morning sitting in a laundromat, reading battered magazines while their stuff went through the wash and dry cycle.

The fog hadn't lifted by noon. It swirled up the streets of Boothbay, engulfing everything in its path. The excursion cruise boats stayed at their moorings. "I don't want to ride in this shit," Cy said. "You can't judge distances worth a damn."

Out in the sea the great buoys sounded deep oooh-oooh, oooh-ooohs. Like death itself, Nat thought. They waited it out, wandering up and down the gray streets and through shops baited for tourists.

The next morning they started out through rising billows of fog. Trees, the rear ends of giant trucks took shape in front of them, suddenly achieving mass and density and then disappearing again. Taillights glowed like warning eyes. The asphalt was slick with salt and grease. They rode slowly, on the alert. By noon the sun burned through, and the Maine coast redeemed itself.

When they took a break, they sat on the guard wall of a scenic lookout and looked down at the deep finger of sea cutting into the land. They talked, comparing the merits of one make of bike to another, the relative assets of men and women, the attributes of the world's great pizzas. Gage told them about herself. She had come East from her family's

Colorado ranch the September before, and she would go into her first year as a nursing student that fall. "That's why I got into bikes," she said. "Sometimes the city drives me bananas. I just had to be free."

Another time they flopped in the thick grass of a town park, near a Civil War monument. On another they strolled along a rotting wharf at the sea's edge and watched cormorants dive and surface and shake fish down their long black throats.

Moving along, Nat thought in flashes of high school, the deli, Orient Square. He saw Uncle Joe's face, but he couldn't sustain any real train of thought. Listening to the motor, keeping his eye on the road, flexing his knees, gearing up and down fractured it. At their next break he talked about it, and Cy said, "The road's no place to think, man. You've gotta stick to business. You start on your problems and you're in trouble."

"I'm not stewing about anything," Nat said. "I just want to think over where I've been and find out where I'm going. What's the road for, if you can't do that?"

"The road's the road," Cy said.

"It's got to mean more than that," Gage murmured.

Eating hamburgers in the Home of the Whopper parking lot, they fell to arguing about the meaning of motorcycles. "To men, bikes are substitutes for women," Gage said. "Guys are always giving them girls' names."

"That's not true," Nat said. "I'd call mine Spartacus. I feel like the master of a rebel slave — you know — is it going to kill me or is it going to behave?"

Cy laughed. "You gotta ride more, that's all. Then you'll see it like your woman, a real worthwhile dame."

"See! I told you!"

Cy squinted at her. "What d'ya call yours? Daddy?"

Gage flared instantly. "Mine's like a horse — it's a substitute for a horse."

"And the horse is a substitute for Daddy."

"It is not!" she cried and threw a cupful of crushed ice in Cy's face.

"So that's where you're livin'." Laughing, Cy rubbed the frozen shavings into his hair and beard.

One afternoon they huddled among rocks to shield them from a cold wind and Cy fell to talking about the Duke of the Road. It was the first Gage had heard of him.

"When you look back on it," she said, "what do you think you really learned from the Duke? Have you thought about that?"

Cy stroked his mustache with his thumb and first finger. "Yeh, plenty of times — I guess I'd say the two important things I got from him were motorcycle mechanics and respect."

"How do you mean — respect? Respect for what?" Nat asked.

Cy laughed. "For about everything — a machine, your work, the place you live, how you live, for yourself."

"Respect for women?" Gage asked.

Cy looked at her, squinting, not answering.

Nat thought of Aunt Rose and how Uncle Joe treated her. And he said, "That's pretty much what I got from Uncle Joe. You could have stayed home and learned that. You wouldn't have learned about bikes, you'd have learned how to make a pizza."

"Joe wanted me to be dependent all the time — under his wing. I about suffocated."

"It wasn't that bad," Nat said. "Maybe he eased up after you split or maybe it was just all right with me." He knew it had been. "After you left, I needed a safe place to run for."

"Well, he wasn't my meat," Cy said, "and the Duke wasn't everybody's meat. Ruckus couldn't take him, but he was the best thing that could happen to me."

After a while they talked less of what they had done before they met and more of what they were doing now. Kids came up to them; boys asked about the gear pattern and girls stood silently by. Single males asked them where they had been and where they were going. An older couple told them they had sons traveling somewhere on bikes and hung around looking lonesome. Some people looked at them sideways, others ignored them. The cops kept tabs.

"I'm still waiting for a female to ask me how I got into this," Gage said. "They just stare."

One day they rode to the top of a hill and saw before them a line of motorcycles more than a mile long. The entire stretch of visible road was covered with them. Like a giant motorized caterpillar they sped toward the sea.

"Like lemmings!" Gage cried. "They're going to throw themselves in."

"It's another of those rites of bikers you never know about," Nat said.

"I'm for findin' out." Cy zoomed ahead.

"Mister Loose." Gage yelled and pulled out, Nat followed.

There were cops at the intersection holding back the cars on both sides as the bikers streamed through. They waved the trio into the line. Cy was laughing as he pulled in. The next moment Nat rode beside a trim older man in brown leathers. "You going somewhere?"

"Yeauh."

"What is this, anyway?"

"The biggest lobster feed you ever saw, that's what it is."

"Free?"

"This is Maine, son."

"Any extras for latecomers?"

"Wouldn't be at all surprised, not at all."

They had started from Augusta and wound their way over the two-lane roads to the sea at Owl's Head. In a little park there on the bluff above the stony shore, great tubs of seawater boiled over charcoal fires, and the huge green claws of lobsters thumped against the sides as they died and turned red. There was plenty of everything for four hundred people, beer and coleslaw and melted butter and potato salad and oversized brownie squares and coffee steaming in great pots and more beer.

"I'm trying to learn to like this stuff," Nat said, popping a can.

"I guess you have to. It's so cheap. Out in Colorado where I come from we have Coors and you don't have to learn to like that."

"Colorado's got some good things," Cy said. "Those mountains —"

"You can see the peaks from our ranch, a little row of triangles about so high. They're like some kind of promise. My father always calls them his reminder."

"Reminder of what?" Nat asked.

"I don't know. He just says they keep him reminded."

"I suppose living right here on the edge of the sea would keep you reminded, like there's something bigger than you are that's going to live longer and be here when you're not."

"It'd be a lot the same," Gage said.

And Cy said, "It reminds me there's a hell of a lot of world out there on the other side of the mountains and the sea that makes me want to keep ridin'."

"You really do hang loose," Gage said, laughing.

They walked around and talked with some of the other cyclists. Nat stood by while a BM man connected a new throttle cable. A couple of Indian collectors chatted beside their antique machines.

Everyone had hit the road by four o'clock. Nat and Gage and Cy stayed on, raking the dumped coals together and heaping on driftwood against the encroaching chill until the flames leaped like a signal fire above the sea.

I'd like this to last forever, Nat thought, the three of us — just like this. He guessed it couldn't, though, watching the flames lick the logs, it wouldn't, maybe even shouldn't.

Anyway, it didn't.

Part Three

BRINGING IT
TOGETHER

≝24≝
Close to
Trouble

Bad guys win first.

— Anonymous

The next day trouble began. Cyrus was irritable. "Are you a woman or aren't you?" Cy snarled at Gage.

"I don't have to do anything I don't want to do."

"She's right," Nat said.

"Whose side are you on?"

"Hers."

Cy swore obscenely. "Wait'll your goddam machine breaks down. Then we'll make a deal."

Nat wasn't sure which one he swore at, angry and nervous as he packed his bike. They were dependent on Cy, his know-how, his experience. Now they were up against his demands. For a moment Nat wished Gage were another guy. There might be tensions but they'd be different. He'd been with a couple of girls, mostly to find out if he could do it and what sex was like, and he'd spent some night hours imagining being with Gage. But a demand — a deal — I fix your machine, you give me a ———. With Gage! Her of all girls! It was infuriating, insulting. It couldn't happen, he hoped.

Then they fell to arguing about where they were going.

"This coast is beautiful. I want to go on north," Gage said. It was all right with Nat. It was beautiful. Even the fog. But Cy had had enough of the rural life. His bike didn't paddle good, he said, so he was as far east as he could go. And race weekend in Loudon, New Hampshire, was coming. He was up for it.

"I like this," Nat argued, not wanting to go looking for more trouble, and Gage said, "I've had it on bike racing like for the rest of my life."

"You haven't seen anything like this. This isn't kids riding motocross. This is road racing. The best in the world will be there. Dick Mann, Gary Nixon, Kenny Roberts — the greatest. I'm goin'."

"But that's in the middle of New Hampshire. We've been there."

"It'll take a couple of days to make it — unless I'm alone." Cyrus fired and throttled his machine, listening to its inner thrum.

"Damn him," Nat muttered.

"The big shit," Gage said. "I hope he throws his chain." She braided her red-brown hair into a long pigtail as she sat astride her bike, then settled her green MS. AMERICA helmet in place, hit the electric start, and shifted into first. Nat waited, watching her, and got going when she did. Cy was already out of sight.

They took Route 3 west toward Augusta. The day sparkled, cool and clear, a perfect day for the road. The winding blacktop rolled over hills, through villages called Liberty and China, passed crystal blue lakes, and went on into the capital.

Cy waited for them in a Merit station. He lounged against his bike, his arms crossed and his legs thrust out, as if he had been there for hours. Nat was fatigued from the road and from the tension. Gage didn't show any weariness. Exchanges were tart. After five minutes they went on.

Farther down the road they were riding fairly close together, Cy leading, Nat and Gage abreast, when Cy slowed and swung to the edge of the pavement. He leaned forward, listening as he shifted down. Then he accelerated again, listening, shifting up through the pattern. After another mile he pulled off.

"What's the matter?" Nat pulled up beside him.

"Hear that tick-tick? That's either the push rod or the roller bearings."

"What do you want to do?"

"Get someplace where I can adjust the push rod. That may do it."

"Next time get a real freedom machine," Gage said, and Cy growled, "Little Honda-ridin' bitch."

"We've got time." Nat pulled the map from inside his denim jacket. "Where do you want to go? Lewiston's down the road. That looks pretty big."

"How far is it? If it's the needle bearings, I don't want them to get into the crankcase."

They rolled into Lewiston and found a Harley dealer. Cy tried to talk him into letting him do his own work, but he wouldn't go along. He would, however, get right at it. By closing time the push rod had been adjusted. They set out again. The tick-tick had gone, and they rode until dark.

The next morning it was back, a nasty nagging little sound they all noticed now.

"This is Thursday," Gage said. "We'll miss the races at this rate." Cyrus swore. "Well, I don't give a damn about them anyway. You're the one who wanted to go."

Nat studied the map. There were no nearby big towns, only more villages called Naples and Limerick.

"I can't go anywhere without gettin' this fixed. There's no two ways about it."

Cy limped into the next town, Steep Falls, with Gage and Nat cruising at twenty-five mph. Nat felt the difference and realized how far he'd come. His feel for the bike was becoming second nature.

They stopped in a gas station, but there was no mechanic and the attendant didn't know of any. Nat suspected the man didn't like their looks. They found an auto shop in a tumbledown garage with wrecks strewn on both sides, but it handled only body work. A man there told them to look up Henry Dysart in Limington. He could fix anything this side of Cape Canaveral. They limped onward, Nat and Gage giving Cy protective cover on the road, and found Henry Dysart standing in front of his barn watching for them.

"That's either the push rod or the roller bearings, son." Only he said "rollah bearin's," being a Maine man.

"I've adjusted the push rod twice."

"Then it's the rollah bearin's. Don't go anothah inch till I fix it. It'll take me a coupla days but you can camp right heah and go into Portland for parts."

"We were up for the races in Loudon," Nat said. "Any chance of hurrying the operation?"

"None at all," Henry said. "You'll just have to miss them this yeah."

"We can double up," Gage said. "Cy can ride behind me." She smiled a secret smile, and Cy squinted viciously back.

"I don't want to miss them," she said sweetly. "I don't know where I'll be next year, but probably not here."

Nat watched his brother carefully. Would a man in black leathers get off a Harley 74 and ride behind a girl on a Honda 500? Would Cyrus ride behind Gage?

"I can carry the gear," he said and waited.

Cy walked around and stretched. He took off his helmet and rubbed his beard. After talking further with Henry, he turned on Nat. "What the hell are you waitin' for? Get the gear on your bike. She can't take both me and it."

They repacked the bikes. The tent and Gage's duffel bag went on Nat's machine so that only one bag was left for Gage. Some stuff they left behind. When they set out again, two machines abreast on the blacktop road, Nat rode inside and Gage outside. Behind her Cy sat back against the bag, inscrutable behind his goggles. Gage laughed all the way to New Hampshire.

≋25≋
Closer

The challenge is — are you going to keep it or are you going to throw it away?

— Bryar

By evening they rolled into Wolfeboro. While they ate in a McDonald's, it grew dark. Nat was for waiting until morning to go on. No night bike riding was a primary rule. But Cy insisted. He said he'd drive, but Gage said the hell he would. No one but she herself was going to handle her machine. Then she broke into gales of laughter. Even Cy smiled, and Nat thought, It takes quite a guy to do what he's doing.

They dropped down to Alton at the foot of Lake Winnepesaukee. There the road streamed with motorcycles, bikes by the tens, the dozens, clubs, groups, singles and doubles. The trio fell into the stream.

They flowed northwest along the lakeshore — a good blacktop road winding in long left-hand and then right-hand bends. Nat found he simply followed the taillight ahead, and he had to dispel consciously the rigidity from fatigue, the tunnel vision creeping over him. They took a break in the Gunstock Recreation Area.

"I want to stop," Gage said.

Cy said, "We keep goin'."

"Sadist!" she snarled, firing her machine. Cy got back on.

They picked up Route 3 and cruised through the main street of Weirs Beach and Lakeport and into Laconia. A few townspeople still sat out in their driveways and on their front steps to watch the parade. The motels on the water flashed NO VACANCY signs. Big road bikes stood in clusters outside the rooms.

"They have beds in there!" Nat yelled. "Real beds!"

"Keep goin'," Cy yelled.

The road turned south again. Route 3 went west and they picked up 106. Then they began to pass campfires. The roadside grew thick with campers. Bikes were parked on the shoulder, with their tails to the ditch, and bikers stood beside them, in front of them, their faces illuminated in headlights, the beer cans in their hands gleaming briefly.

"Look for a high place — back from the road," Cy yelled.

"How? It's pitch dark!"

"Keep lookin'."

They passed Bryar's Motorsport Park, the track dark and silent behind high board fences. In the distance a few lights reflected off vans and campers in the paddock. They rode on. Bystanders yelled at them, "Pop a wheelie!" followed by a burst of laughter. They crowded in so close that Nat and Gage had to go single file. Farther on a great crowd had gathered in front of a general store. Beyond that there was a pine grove turned into a campground. Banners fluttered beside the road — gang colors. "Keep goin'," Cy ordered.

"I'm dead!" Gage cried out. "We've gotta find a place."

"Not here," Cy said.

"I think I saw a good place up an embankment back there about a mile," Nat said. "How about going back?"

They made U-turns, using the side road to the Easy Rider Cycle Shop, and retraced their way. They passed the general store again and found a place where the highway had been cut through a shoulder of a hill. A grassy dirt track led up to a flat area where some guys were already camped. They rode on another thirty feet or so, still climbing, and found a second plateau with just enough room for them and screened somewhat by a thicket of scrub birches. Gage said, "Here — no farther."

They pulled the two bikes up on the center stands, fumbled with the bungee cords until they loosened, threw their sleeping bags out, and, ignoring the howls from the roadside, crawled in. Nat listened, briefly thinking he was missing something; then he caught a whiff of dope.

"Breathe deep. It's free." Cy laughed.

Nat took in the fragrance, tense and apprehensive but too exhausted to think.

Before sunrise the next morning somebody beside the road began to yell at his companions, "Get the ——— up." Nat rolled onto his back, his eyelids gummed closed. After a while the guy called out, "Good morning!" sweetly, and from down the road the answer came just as sweetly, "Good morning!" Then he fired a machine noisier than any Nat had ever heard, rode it among the tents, over tent pegs, under front flaps, throttling outside open van doors. For five minutes he ripped the gray dawn apart, and then turned it off. No one could be left asleep, but the silence was heavy. Then someone called out, "Must be a Norton," and laughter hooted from tents here and there. Nat looked at his watch. Six-thirty.

"Nat, do you have anything to eat?" Gage asked. "I could chew my leathers."

"I don't even have leathers."

The camp below them began to stir.

"How are we going to go into town and leave our stuff here? And if we take our stuff, we'll lose our place."

Nat pulled on his blue jeans and jacket and rode back to the general store where a crowd had already gathered, already popping beer cans as they stood around waiting for it to open. A cop in a cruiser beckoned him over and asked him about his club, where were the Brothers of the Open Road located? He said, "Boston," and grinned. "We're straight."

"And that ain't everybody that's here," the cop said. "This is a bad scene."

Nat didn't reply. His stomach contracted into a hard ball, and the old wariness prickled over him. He glanced around. Everybody looked raunchy, denims spattered with road grease, grime sticking to that, big heads of hair matted and sweaty from helmets, beer cans held at belt level. It was only eight A.M. If it was bad now, it would get worse.

"Big crowd?" he asked.

"They figure ten thousand by last night. And more coming."

When the store opened, Nat pushed his way in and wandered along the shelves, picking out a package of sweet rolls, a carton of milk and some sugar-coated cereal. He was standing beside his bike, strapping the brown bag on, when he heard the sound of many great road bikes flowing toward him. He looked up. A line of giant white Harleys streamed into sight, 1200s, all of them white. All of them weighted with double panniers and a trunk. All of them ridden double. The group pulled into the open space around the store. Immediately they were the center of attention. Nat left his bike to look. The riders were dressed in matching outfits, men and women, most of them as old as Uncle Joe and Aunt Rose. They wore immaculate yellow jackets with "Riders of the Golden State" across the back. Even their hair didn't look too bad as they eased their helmets off. Nat pressed through the onlookers for a closer look. Every exposed part on every bike was fully chromed. There were so many taillights they were arranged like wickets, in triangles. He counted twenty-six on one, and he was still counting. Tucked behind the fairing, each machine carried a tape deck and a radio and a microphone for two-way communication on the road. He laughed in amazement and exchanged wondering glances with the guy next to him.

"This freaks me out," he said.

There was only one oddball bike in the bunch, and it was still a Harley, but an old one, the heavy fenders their original purple. It carried a solitary rider, much trimmer gear, and the motor had the sound of perfect tuning. The rider, a black man, came to a halt and surveyed the crowd. He looked at Nat, pushed up his goggles, and let his gaze travel down to Nat's boots. Suddenly Nat felt sweaty and crusty. He turned back to his bike and set off. The road had narrowed to little more than one wide lane. Cars had trouble passing, although bikes made it easily. The ditches were rapidly filling with trash, mostly cans. Nat shifted down and climbed the hill to their campsite.

Cy and Gage had pitched the little orange tent. Gage brushed her dark red hair over her head while Cy swished his mouth with a guzzle from his canteen.

Nat tilted his bike on the sidestand and hung his helmet on the handlebar. He tossed an orange at each of them.

"I saw —" he began, " — you won't believe what I saw — well, maybe you would — they're from California — a whole bunch —"

Cy wiped his mouth on the tail of his T-shirt. "On white 1200s?"

Nat nodded. "Fully chromed, with —"

"Yellow jackets — the Riders of the Golden State?"

"Running lights like — God! And two-way radios!"

"Was there another guy with them —"

"Two-way radios!"

"On an old purple Harley?"

"A black guy?"

Cy whooped. "He came! I knew he would!"

"Who came?"

"The Duke! That's the Duke!"

"The Duke! Is the Duke a black guy?"

"Yeh, where is he?"

"They're at the store down the road, out they're headed this way, I guess. They came up 106 from the other end."

Cy was already sliding down the embankment toward the road. Nat and Gage looked at each other. She was clean. She had on the better of her two pairs of jeans and a tank top. Nat began to rummage in his pack. Damn. His other pants were just as bad, his T-shirts grungey, just when cleanliness was about to count. The air hummed with the sound of the oncoming bikes.

⚌26⚌
Meeting the Duke

Let the good times roll!

— Phoebe Snow

The giant bikes came around the bend as Cy hit the shoulder of the road. The leader pointed toward Cy and raised his hand. Behind him the others slewed to the side, turned off, calling out. "It's Cyrus!"

A moment later the Duke came in sight. Cy held out his thumb like a hitchhiker. The purple Harley came to a full stop. The Duke put his forearm across his eyes as if he couldn't believe what he saw.

Nat and Gage watched from their perch on top of the bank. Cy pointed up to them, then he got on behind and the Duke headed the bike up the hill toward them. The others went on their way.

As soon as he settled his machine, the Duke got off — and he was a huge man, a regular Jimmy Brown, Nat thought, big and getting a little soft at the belt but not much. He stood up and hugged Cy and Cy hugged him. Several times they tightened their arms around each other. "Oh, man, you look good, you do look good," the Duke exclaimed.

"This is my brother, Nat."

"I told him to go look for you," the Duke said. Nat shook hands, a little atom of understanding bursting in his stomach. "And this is Gage — we found her along the road."

"Beautiful! Beautiful! Is this where you're camping?"

Nat looked around quickly to see if the camp would meet inspection. "We just got here last night," he murmured, in case anything looked out of place. "We're about to eat breakfast."

"You go ahead. I've eaten. If you've got any coffee, I'll take some." The Duke frowned when he saw their breakfast. "You're not eating right. Too much sweet stuff."

Gage boiled some water on the one-burner stove and gave him a cup of coffee. "That does smell good!" He smiled at her and slipped out of his jacket, laying it over his bike. It was a beautiful coat, cinnamon brown leather cut like a Barbour jacket, with side vents, and topstitched in black by hand. All the zippers were covered with flaps so that they didn't show.

"You got through all right?" he asked Cy, who said he had. He told him about George Pepperall's funeral, and the Duke listened without moving. "Is Ruckus here?"

"I haven't seen him. I was going to find their camp later on."

"Not with her, I hope."

"When I left, you weren't so sure you'd make it this year," Cy said.

Stirring his coffee, the Duke said, "You know how it is — it's a big race. I entered maybe six times in the fifties and broke a chain or lost power or some damn thing every time. I've got this unfulfilled tug over this race. Then the Golden Staters decided to come and a couple others, so we hit the road. We're taking a motel on the lake."

Cy and the Duke brought out their cigarettes. Although the mood seemed relaxed, the Duke's face grew darker.

"There's going to be trouble, Cyrus. This is a bad scene. I feel it coming."

"I don't feel anything — not yet, anyway."

"I'm an old hand at sensing trouble."

"I've seen my share," Cyrus said, "but I don't —"

"Listen," said the Duke.

They fell silent, listening to the raucous sound of bikes coming up the road. The noise split the air as three bikes went past. The forks were so extended the riders' feet were propped up level with their knees. One rider downed the last of a beer and the can went bouncing and ringing on the asphalt. At that moment a waft of dope breezed upward from the camp below.

The Duke's wide nostrils widened. "That's what I mean — trouble."

Cyrus had nothing to say, and Nat felt a nervous prickle move up his neck into his hair. He thought, I can split, but he didn't really want to. He didn't want to leave Gage and Cy — or the Duke, either. There were four of them, if the Duke stayed with them. Sweat dampened his armpits, and he knew he was scared, but not a whole lot, and he thought, God! I've come a long way!

"Where's your machine?" the Duke asked Cyrus.

"The roller bearing finally went and I had to leave it with a guy in Maine. It won't be ready till next week. I have to go back for it."

From there they went into an esoteric discussion of push rods and needle bearings. Nat sat on the edge of the bank, peeling an orange and watching the road. It was thick with bikes. In the distance the speaker system at the track made announcements he couldn't quite understand. Bikes whined in rising and falling decibels, coming and going away, as their riders made practice runs. It was hot, the sky opaque, the sun cooking through.

Gage sat down beside him. "You know, we're in a good spot," she said. "If there's a riot, we can just watch."

"And run like hell if we have to." Nat laughed, not knowing then that soon one of them would be doing just that.

Below them the traffic was bumper to bumper. Cars were suddenly stuck going both ways, some of them headlight to headlight. It looked like a four laner because those who had taken to the shoulder were stopped as dead as the mainstream. Bikes whined and roared in and out. A siren began to scream behind them. The cars pressed aside, scraping metal, and a little ambulance bus squeezed through along the center line. Following it came a heavy pickup, in the back a mangled and twisted bike.

Gage turned pale. "Oh, Jesus," Nat groaned. He felt every nerve, every sensing system in his body spring to alert. You know you're alive when you're in the presence of death.

The siren died away, and some sort of commotion erupted in the other direction. Horns blared. Great shouts and cheers broke out. Suddenly coming toward them across the car tops, leaping from roof to hood to roof, came a naked runner, a banner fluttering from his right hand.

Bikers and bystanders howled encouragement. A police cruiser tried to get loose to follow him but couldn't. One of the officers got out and began to press through the stalled cars. The crowd howled encouragement to him, too, but before he came close, the streaker jumped off, stumbled through the ditch at the side of the road, and disappeared into the woods.

Slowly the cars began to move.

Cy and the Duke stood beside them.

"I didn't know these races drew so many people," Gage exclaimed.

"They aren't here for the races." The Duke's mouth pulled down with disgust.

"Most of them'd like to see a lot of bikers get creamed or arrested or watch the Angels beat up the cops," Cy said. "They don't know who Gary Nixon is."

"Well, who is he?" Gage asked.

"Yeh, who is he?" asked Nat, but he didn't listen to the answer. He watched while a knot of six bikers passed something from hand to hand which drew them intently together. Every few seconds one raised his head to scan the highway and the crowd. Were they selling stuff? He didn't see any money changing hands. They must be divvying up, dope or speed or coke or something. The crazy scene was going to get crazier.

The Duke began to pace back and forth, muttering, "Goddam! Goddam! They're lined up and down that highway by the thousands. Nobody's brought in any portable facilities. What the hell are those sponsors thinking about? This state's going to be uninhabitable by Sunday night. What do they expect people to do?" His voice was angry. "It's stupid, and you know who's going to get the blame?"

They knew, they knew.

"I hate to see it!" the Duke exclaimed. "And the trash — the littering's already started. Cy, you be sure to carry this stuff out of here when you leave, you hear? I hate to see bikers get a bad name." He looked at his watch. "I want to get to the track before the qualifying trials start. I didn't come all the way from L.A. just for a traffic jam."

"I'll go with you," Cy said.

"I will, too," Gage said, and Nat thought, the track is probably the best place to be. They mean business there; you knew which way the action would go. Here anything could happen. He gave his machine a quick visual check, stomped on the starter, and rocked his helmet down on his head. The Duke fired his Harley.

"I'll ride with you, Duke. Okay?" Cy said.

The Duke nodded. They zipped up their jackets, and Cy took the seat behind him. A moment later and they were caught in the traffic on 106. It was much, much worse than early that morning. They managed to edge into the flow when a car stalled and couldn't get started. The bystanders pressed in so tight that the road wasn't even one lane wide. They moved for a few minutes and then came to a dead stop. Five minutes, maybe more went by. Nothing moved.

"What's happened?" They shouted to oncoming drivers.

"Another accident," Gage said.

"We'll never get to the track," the Duke growled.

Then they were distracted by the appearance of the weirdest, wildest machine to make the scene. Coming toward them was a tricycle, no, it was a quadricycle. A great extended fork bike was flanked by two VW wheels. Four people rode it. The driver gripped the high narrow handlebars with someone on behind him, while two others rode the outrigger wheels on

seats with high padded backs and high foot-pegs. The crowd
lining the ditches and in the vehicles cheered and honked as it
passed, and the riders acknowledged with royal waves of their
hands.

Nat called out to another biker, "What's going on up
there?"

"They're drag racing, but the cops are breaking it up."

"We want to get to the track," Cy yelled.

"Good luck!" the biker called back.

꩜27꩜
Qualifying
Heat

*If you ever helped a fellow rider, you
paid your dues in the biking brotherhood.*

— Anonymous

They moved forward for two minutes, stalled again, then crawled on. Another five minutes and the sign for Bryar's Motorsport Park rose ahead of them on the right. The Duke cut off into an open field where a couple of hundred campers and vans were parked. Nat followed, threading his way through the parked vehicles to the racetrack entrance. The Duke paid for the four of them. They shouted protests, but he waved them off.

There was a guarded area set aside for motorcycle parking. They left the three bikes there and walked along the edge of the track toward the pits. A few racers took their bikes around the course. Nat stopped at the fence to watch as a 125 Yamaha shrieked into the turn. It had a narrow, rounded, racing fairing cut away for the handlebars, and a straight, narrow body with a cut-in seat. The rider's bright green leathers matched his machine. Coming into the turn, he leaned out to the right. Nat saw how he cocked his right leg, his knee almost touching the track, and as he came out of the turn, he snapped upright and tucked his body low behind the fairing.

Cy was yelling at him. Nat left the fence and moved on.

Because of the Duke's connections they were admitted to the paddock where the racers and their crews prepared, and they saw Gary Nixon, Gary Scott, Gary Fisher — "Do racers have to be called Gary?" Gage asked — Kenny Roberts and Dick Mann and Gene Romero.

"Not Italian," Cy said. Near their crews the racers waited, their leather jumpsuits zipped down in the heat, their wire-thin bodies at ease without being easy, their eyes inward and intense. The crews worked. Engines screamed and whined, and the tension was contagious.

Cyrus stopped here and there to talk to guys he knew from California. Nat noticed how they greeted him with pleasure and pounded his arm.

"Is this your first race?" a mechanic asked Nat, who said it was. "This is my third," he said. "If you can stand the noise, you'll be hooked." They laughed, and Nat felt the excitement of the inside workings get to him. Cy gripped his shoulder as they walked along the narrow lane between the rows and yelled into his ear, "I told you a National's worth the trouble."

"What trouble?" They laughed, and Cy slapped his shoulder.

Suddenly behind them someone was shouting, "Duke! Cyrus! Hey!" and a man appeared from a side lane and took Duke's arm. "We're havin' trouble — bad trouble — with Dave's machine — the goddam choke —" They were already moving toward some racer's place in the pits. The Duke's face became absorbed, Cy's listening. Nat followed with Gage.

Three crews down from the corner where the lanes met, two men stood beside a small Harley 250 fitted with racing fairing and narrow, straight handlebars and a cut-in seat the size and shape of a brick. They stared at it, their arms hanging at their sides, helpless and threatening. The racer watched them, his leathers rolled down to his waist. His torso was so thin and pale that even the swelling muscles didn't erase its vulnerability. Sweat trickled from his curling hair.

The Duke threw him his jacket. "Let's see this choke." He got on the bike, dwarfing it beneath him, and tried to fire the machine. Cy leaned toward him. The starter refused to catch, and the Duke began questioning the two mechanics.

Cy signed to Nat. "You'd better go get some seats in the stands before they fill up. We're goin' to be here awhile."

They left the paddock for the stands along the front straightaway. Nat and Gage found seats, trying to hold space for Cy and the Duke. When they were settled, Nat went behind the stands to buy a barbecued chicken and a couple of beers. Back in his seat, a can in one hand, a quarter-chicken in the other, Nat wondered if he had ever felt better. Gage was next to him, some of her dark reddish hair secured at the back of her head, wonderfully lithe and slender and exposed in her tank T-shirt — a really beautiful and different girl, he meant female, that is, woman.

She turned to him, smiling. "Look at them, Nat. They look like spacemen."

He laughed. They did, a little. The racers stood beside their machines in the track below, their leather jumpsuits emphasizing lean tense bodies, the wraparound cannonball helmets obscuring their faces and personalities. It was a Le Mans start, and the racers lined up against the wall opposite their bikes, waited for the flag, then sprinted to the machines, leaped on, and gunned them into the front stretch.

"I've been in horse shows where we had to mount like that," Gage shrieked over the noise.

It was a race of production machines, standard factory-built models without modifications for racing: 750s, 1000s, just like those anybody would take on the road. Watching them, Nat thought any biker could learn some fine points. He rooted for a solitary BM entrant and Gage shrieked for the big Hondas, but after a couple of laps it was obvious the Kawasakis and Ducatis had the race to themselves.

A light breeze spread clouds across the sky. Rain swept the track, coming and going in a few minutes. The trial heats were halted until the track dried. White cement powder was scattered on the wettest places. The spectators who had left the stands when it sprinkled surged back. Not a seat was left. When the Duke appeared, they had to squeeze him in.

"Did you find the trouble?" Nat asked.

"Cyrus did." The Duke looked enormously pleased. "He's got know-how in his fingertips. He's beautiful."

An inner fire warmed Nat, and he smiled.

Before the Duke was well settled, a squadron of shrieking 125s left the starting line. They were bunched up at first, but by the first curve they began to string out. The track swung left, then right, then left. The bikes picked up speed on a straight stretch, made a right-angle, right-hand turn, and whined uphill at 100 mph.

After that race a platoon of 250s left the pits, all of them mounted by their riders and pushed by their tuners. Cyrus pushed Dave. The racers lined up four abreast in rows across the track. Dave had drawn a front row place. The official gave the signal to start motors. The little engines screamed and puffed white smoke. All but Dave's.

"Goddam!" the Duke exclaimed, standing up. Cy bent over the machine. "Come on, Cy!" Nat yelled. Cy pushed Dave out in front, but he couldn't spark it. Gage shrieked encouragement. They turned the bike and Cy pushed it at a run back toward the lineup. No puff of exhaust. The seconds ticked away. Cy ran it as fast as he could to the rear. Still no go. Dave jumped off, and Cy piled on. Nat shook his fist. "Come on! Fire, dammit!" And it fired. Cy throttled, holding it for Dave, who got on as Cy slid off. A second later the machine found its slot, and the green flag came down. Nat roared, shaking his fist in the air.

"What'd I tell you?" the Duke yelled. "He's somethin' else."

Nat threw back his head and shouted for joy. They yelled at each other, embraced, shook hands, and shook their fists in the air.

The screaming bikes fled up the hill on the back-straight, taking the deep turn banked with old tires, went down the straight into a hairpin, back along the far side of the pond, into curve #10 along the paddock and onto the front-straight. Going into each curve the rider slid sideways out of the seat, his leg cocked, his knee almost scraping the asphalt. As his machine sped onto the straight, he eased back and tucked his body low behind the fairing. You could hear them shifting in and out of the turns, the engines shrieking like witching winds.

"They're beautiful!" Gage exclaimed, almost breathless.

Nat laughed. Oh, he felt good! good! good! If these were

just the qualifying heats, what would the finals be like on Sunday?

Or would there be any Sunday race? Suddenly it was raining again, heavily this time, and the flagmen waved the racers off the track. This time they took shelter under the stands. Again it cleared. The cement powder was sprinkled on the oil spills. The watchers surged back and forth, cursing irritably and guzzling more beer.

"This is more like punishment," the Duke muttered.

When Cy appeared, they decided to split, but leaving wasn't easy. The gates were choked with cars and bikes, going both ways, and outside the gate the highway and its shoulders up and down as far as you could see were jammed. The Duke took the lead, turning back toward their camp. Gage stalled out for a minute, and they lost their chance to follow. Nat edged out into the road, forced an opening, and they roared across the north-bound lane, taking the center line. They caught up because Cy and the Duke were snared in traffic. This time the traffic did not move. Five minutes they waited, ten, longer.

"What the hell?" Cy said. "Let's leave 'em here and walk up there and find out what's happenin'."

The Duke said, "I'm not going out of sight of this machine — not in this bunch. They'd take a throttle for a souvenir."

Papers and beer cans were strewn everywhere. An occasional breath of warm air brought the stink of excrement. "See what I mean?" the Duke said. "This state will be unfit for human life by morning."

"They just didn't expect the crowd," Gage said.

"They should have. They advertised all over the country."

The Duke was angry and worried. "Damn them, damn them," he muttered.

Nat wasn't sure whom he damned, bikers or sponsors or thrill-seeking crowds.

A great cheer went up ahead. Leaving the bikes, they pressed through the onlookers. The cheering doubled and tripled. A great chorus of honks joined in.

"What's going on?" Nat asked of no one and everyone. He moved into a vacant space on the bank's edge, and there below him he saw.

Three naked young men strutted beside the stalled cars. Their shirts and jeans were strewn along the shoulder, and they had only their bike boots on. One of them had picked up a stick and twirled it like a baton. They strutted toe-heel toe-heel like drum majorettes on parade. When their leader did an about-face, they all turned and came toward Nat.

Their faces were glazed, their eyes curiously empty and dull, and he groaned. They were high on something, maybe a couple of things. He sucked his breath through his teeth.

"Damn them! Damn them!" the Duke swore. "Look at that little girl!"

Then Nat noticed the passengers in the car. Two women stared in horror through the closed window, and from the back seat a little girl's face appeared, her round eyes popping.

The next thing Nat knew, the Duke had jumped from the bank into the ditch. He strode angrily, his great size menacing in itself, toward the naked offenders.

"They're stoned!" Cy yelled. "Leave them!" But the Duke either didn't hear him or didn't want to stop. He strode toward the three as they wheeled and strutted beside the jammed cars.

Nat and Gage began to laugh hysterically while the strutters tossed their long hair and marked time with their right hands — oompah-oompah across their bare bellies — and toe-heeled in line along the shoulder. The Duke came up behind them and grabbed one by his ponytail and turned him around.

"Look out!" Cy yelled, but it was too late. The broken bottle arced overhead, struck the Duke on the side of the head, and splintered again. Blood gushed instantly from his scalp. He let go the ponytail and put his hand to his head. As he lowered his hand, dripping red, he crumpled to his knees.

Someone in a car began screaming. Nat heard Cy cursing as they ran toward the Duke, but when they knelt beside him, only he and Gage were there.

"We've got to get him to a hospital," Gage cried.

Not a car could move. Gage tried to stop the bleeding while Nat stood up. Six cars down the line was a VW bug. He ran to it and leaned in the window and cried, "Somebody's hurt. Can you get loose? We've got to get him to a hospital." The driver backed and turned and turned and backed until he had made a U and roared back to the spot where the Duke lay.

"One of us has got to stay with the bikes," Nat said. "You go. I'll wait here."

Heaving a man as big as the Duke, now all dead weight, into a VW took three of them.

"Where's Cyrus?" Gage gasped, as she tried to lift one leg.

"I thought he was with us," Nat said. With the driver, they lifted and heaved and pushed and finally fitted the big man into the passenger seat.

"You go with him!" Nat cried out. "I'll find Cyrus." Gage scrambled into the back seat before the driver got in, snatched up a newspaper from the floor and pressed it against the Duke's deep slash. Blood was still streaming from it and had splashed on the car, on all of them.

"Sorry," Nat said.

"Forget it," the driver said. "Come on."

"I have to stay with the bikes," Nat said. "I'll find Cyrus and we'll get to the hospital. Wait for us, Gage."

He stepped back. Beeping hysterically, the little bug inched its way through the traffic.

Nat turned to the crowd on the bank and scanned it. "Did you see the guy who was with me?" No one answered. "Brown beard. Black leathers." Half the people on the bank had brown beards and black leathers. Nat scrambled up and began to walk back toward their machines. Just wait there, he thought. Cy knows where they are.

Then suddenly Cy appeared. Two state troopers had him by each arm, and they hustled him from the woods down the bank and into a cruiser. For one second Nat stood stunned. Then he jumped down and ran, yelling, "That's my brother!"

The trooper gave him an elbow in the stomach that set him back gasping.

"They think I did it!" Cy yelled from the middle of the back seat.

"Shut up," a trooper snarled.

"He didn't do anything," Nat yelled. "He's Duke's friend."

"Some friend!" They piled into the cruiser, glaring back at Nat, set the blue light and the siren going. In a few seconds space opened before them, and the spinning blue light and a shrieking siren marked its passage through the jam.

28

Barred
Doors

Freedom's just another word
for nuthin' left to lose.

— Janis

Oh, God, Nat moaned, now what am I going to do? He couldn't ride three bikes at once. He couldn't leave them without running a big risk. And he couldn't stay with them and help Cy.

Nat stood on the edge of the bank, frowning and chewing his lip and staring at the traffic. It moved a little, and a squadron of bikers came in sight. His stomach knotted. It was the Angels. The narrow passage widened. The crowd moved back, giving them plenty of room.

Nat jumped into the ditch and stepped out on the shoulder in front of the crowd. "Ruckus!" he yelled.

The lead rider turned his mirror sunglasses toward him, staring and then recognizing him. He stopped, and the others behind him pulled up. Nat stood beside Ruckus and explained. Ruckus nodded, sure, one of the guys could stay with the bikes and he'd ferry Nat back from his camp.

"The traffic's —" Nat searched for a word, but Ruckus said,

"They're gettin' out of the way pretty good." He looked over the purple Harley. "That the Duke's?"

"Some friend of Cy's," Nat muttered, not wanting to tell Ruckus the whole story. He might take the resolution into his own hands. "What's the gear pattern, Ruckus? I've never ridden a Harley."

He rode Duke's machine to the camp and parked it behind the tent. Ruckus ferried him back for Gage's bike.

"Who's this Mzz America?" he asked. Nat didn't answer, cussing and concentrating on the Honda gears which were on the right, the opposite of the BM's. When he had stowed it beside the Duke's, Ruckus gave him a lift back to his own machine.

Meanwhile, the Angels had just waited in the middle of the highway. No one asked them to move.

Nat rode with them as far as the entrance to their camp. It was the fastest way to get through the traffic. There the Angels turned off, and Nat and Ruckus exchanged raised fists.

Sweating with relief, Nat continued toward Laconia. He tried to thread through the lanes of traffic, but just as he got going into the open, some biker would appear coming toward him. There was no room to pass. Everyone was cursing foully. Car drivers called out, "What's the matter up ahead?" Nat shrugged; he didn't know. It was the same for miles ahead, and behind him.

When he stopped sweating, he began to laugh. Getting a few Hell's Angels to guard the bikes — outta sight! Then he fell to swearing again at not being able to get out of first gear. It took him nearly an hour to get into Laconia.

The Laconia police station was located in the old stone railway depot. It took up what had been the main waiting room while the cruisers pulled up under the old covered entrance-way. A small crowd of bikers clustered around the double doors. Nat pulled up his bike at a right angle to the sidewalk and tried to push his way into the station. He was shoved and elbowed.

"Wait your turn, buddy!" someone yelled.

"They've got my brother," Nat said.

"Yeh? They've got my old lady. You know what cops do to a chick."

Suddenly stricken with anxiety, Nat fell back and took his place in line. Thirty minutes passed. He inched forward. By the time the rain stopped, he was inside.

Maybe they had let Cy go already, Nat thought. After a moment's reflection he added to himself, No way.

In another twenty minutes he stood before the desk sergeant and said, "You picked up my brother out on the highway about four o'clock. Cyrus Coombs?"

The sergeant looked at his book. "C-o-o-m-b-s? Gardena, California? We got him."

"I'm his brother."

"So you're his brother."

Nat pulled out his billfold and searched for his driver's license. "I saw what happened. A girl did, too. Mary Gage Weaver from Cheyenne Wells, Colorado. We both saw it. She took the black guy to the hospital. We saw it, and we know Cyrus didn't throw the bottle. He was with us."

"Yeh?" The sergeant listened. "I can't do anything about it. He's booked. He's down on the blotter. He'll be arraigned Monday. The court's right in there. Come back then."

"Monday! That's two days away! You know if you'd call the hospital and get the injured party to testify, this whole thing would get clear in a split second. The Duke knows my brother."

The desk sergeant darkened. "What's your connection with him? You trying to run some poor black down?"

"No!" Nat yelled. "Believe me. Can I see my brother? He'll tell you."

"Once they're booked, they'll tell us anything. I've heard 'em all, sonny."

"I don't want him stuck in jail."

"This place isn't so bad. If you like jail, you'll like it," the desk sergeant said. "But you can get him out on bail."

"How much?" Nat asked.

"Five hundred smackers."

Nat went white. "Why five hundred?"

"Assault with a deadly weapon. Disorderly conduct. Resisting an officer."

"You're really pouring it on!" Nat's face was blood-red with fury. "Can't you think up another charge?"

The desk sergeant stared at him steadily. "I don't have to. I know this judge. There's nothing he'd like better than to teach you dirty bikies a lesson — and this one —" he tapped the book — "this one he's got dead to rights. He won't be traveling again for quite a while."

Nat stepped back as if he had been pushed. The others behind him listened silently and made a path for him. One biker gripped his shoulder. Nat nodded, his mouth dry, his stomach knotted and sick. He pushed out through the doors and sat down on the curb beside his bike, the rain sluicing off his bare head. He didn't have five hundred dollars. Neither did Gage. Cy had a lot of money, but not that much. He studied the rain bouncing off the gutter puddles. He had several hundred in his savings account at home. Uncle Joe was co-signer. He could call him — but Uncle Joe had always hated Cyrus. This would just prove to him that he had been right all along. For a moment Nat felt the warmth of the deli, the familiar old routines of helping his uncle, being sheltered and protected by him. He had left that behind him now. He was on his own. There was only one thing to do — get the Duke to testify right now before Cy faced that hanging judge. Nat stomped on the kick starter, rocked his bike off the stand, and gunned it for the hospital.

≋ 29 ≋

Rescue
Mission

Keep on bikin'.

— Biker's T-shirt

Gage sat in a yellow molded plastic chair in the little hospital's lobby. Her leather jacket was open, and her hair hung over her shoulders in oily, disordered strands. She looked very tired.

"I thought something happened to you." She looked up at Nat without much interest.

"There's blood on your jacket."

She nodded. "Yeh, I know."

"How's the Duke?"

"He's okay. They took x-rays of his head, all that."

"That doesn't sound too good."

"Routine, really."

"I've got to see him. They picked up Cy and charged him with throwing the bottle."

Suddenly Gage sat up and exclaimed, "That's crazy."

"All we need is a word from the Duke that he didn't do it."

"He was discharged an hour ago," Gage cried out.

"What!"

"He split. I told him I'd wait here for you."

"Oh God! Where'd he go?"

"He didn't say — I didn't ask him — but he left his bike back there on the road."

"Yeh! He's got to get his bike. And I moved it. I took it back to the camp. He won't know that —"

"But he'll think of it," Gage said.

"Come on! We've got to get there first."

He fired his machine and got on. Gage flicked out the foot-pegs and settled behind him. Instantly they were off, splashing through the puddles. Gage put her arms around his waist and laid her head against his back. She didn't peek over his shoulder, trying to read the road and second-guess him. She became one with him, leaning when he leaned, part of him, part of the bike. They flew over the roads.

They returned to 106 and went south toward the track. The asphalt was black with rain, although only a few drops still fell. The camps alongside the road were bedraggled. Some had disappeared. Others had rigged up shelters, big sheets of plastic, ripped-down billboards propped on posts. Someone threw gasoline on a fire as they passed, and the flames shot fifty feet in the air. The track was half-deserted, the board fences dark with rain, the stands empty, and the parking lot churned to muck. The crowd had thinned a lot, both kinds of crowd, the serious fans and the funsters. The lines of beer-guzzling bikers had vanished completely. Nat turned up the hillside and gunned the bike through mud and boggy spots up the last few yards to their campsite.

The little orange tent stood there, closed tight. Gage's red

Honda, cleansed by the rain, leaned on its stand beside it. The big purple Harley was gone. Nat sat astride his bike and stared. Where would the Duke go?

"Hey, you." Someone from the camp below stood in the track, yelling at them.

"Did you see anybody take a big purple Harley?" Nat shouted. The man nodded, and Nat turned his bike and rolled downhill toward him. "Was it a big guy — about forty — black?"

"Ridin' with the Angels?" the other fellow asked.

Nat stared at him.

"He came up here with a couple Angels and just took the bike. We saw him, and we didn't know whose bike it was — but, you know, man, we weren't about to ask for proof of ownership." He laughed a little.

"It's his machine all right. I've got to find him. Did you see him ride off with the Angels?"

The fellow rubbed his head. "Naw — they went south."

"And he turned north — toward Laconia? But we just came over that road."

"That was maybe a half hour back."

"We'd have missed him, Nat, the way we came out from the hospital."

"Jesus," Nat muttered. "Where'd he go?"

"He was traveling with those Golden Staters," Gage said. "They were headed for some motel on the lake."

"Right! Right!" They bumped downhill to the highway, and Nat swung north again back toward Laconia. He knew this road by heart now. The rain had broken up the traffic so that he threaded his way through the cars, breaking all the rules, taking the breakdown lane when he could, the center line when he had to. Twenty minutes later they swung through the main streets of Laconia. "Which motel?"

"I don't know — I don't think they said."

The townspeople had brought their lawn chairs out to the curb to watch the evening motorcycle parade. The steps of shops and homes were filled with spectators.

"Have you seen a club on white 1200 Harleys?" Nat called out.

"What?" came the answer.

"They don't know a Harley from a hole in their heads." They sped on.

The motel strip in Lakeport had a dozen establishments on the shore. They cruised up one side and down the other. No giant white Harleys were parked in front of them.

"We've got to ask," Gage yelled.

Nat nodded and pulled into the next motel. Gage slid off. Nat handed her the bike and ran into the office. No one was around. A cardboard sign said SORRY. He pounded a little steel bell, his fury rising.

"Nat! They're here! They're parked around in back!"

Together they ran around the corner of the long low building, where the great white Harleys were parked in a precision row.

"Golden Staters!" Gage cried out. "Is there a Golden Stater here?"

Several doors opened, and two women and a man appeared, questions on their faces.

"We're looking for the Duke —"

"Duke Rhoades?"

"Yeh — I'm Nat Coombs — Cyrus is my brother — and

he's in jail because the cops think he threw the bottle that hit the Duke, and they won't believe me. I'm trying to find the Duke so he can convince them —"

"Oh, that's awful!" one woman said, and the other murmured, "Really terrible."

"I wish I could help you, but the Duke just stopped in to say he'd see us in California. Then he headed out."

"You mean he left town?"

"That's right. He said this was no place for him. He hated everything about it."

"Oh, God!" Nat groaned.

"He hasn't been gone too long," the first woman said. "You may be able to catch up with him. I don't think he's riding too fast. He said he had a terrible headache."

"How long ago —"

"Oh, ten, maybe fifteen minutes."

"Did he say —"

"California is all I can tell you." The man smiled ruefully, making a small helpless gesture. "Look at the map a minute. Maybe we can figure out his route." In a glance it was clear. He'd take 3 down to I-93, but once he was there, only the Duke would know which way he went.

"The Duke has a radio, Judson," the woman said. "You could try to reach him that way. If he has his set on — he can't send — but if he hears you —"

"By George, you're right. I'll try it. You get going, Nat. We'll do what we can from here."

Nat hit the highway, accelerating so fast that Gage almost sailed out behind. He glanced backward an instant, and she said, "Don't worry about me. I'll hang in here."

They raced through the town center. A cruiser pulled out

from a side street, dome light spinning. He was sure he'd get it now. He slowed — he was only ten miles over the speed limit. The cops turned the other way.

Then they were out of town, flying over the darkening road. Gage lay against him, moving with him, balancing with him. He glanced at the dials — God! he was hitting eighty! He shook fear out of his head, remembering the racers tucked behind their fairings on the straight, sliding from their seats on the curves. The orange stripe rolled past his shoulder, shiny, slick as enamel. He stayed well to the right of it.

In front of him loomed a car with New Hampshire plates. "Live Free or Die," the license read. He snorted. There isn't any living free, bikes or no bikes. Everything, he thought, everything has rules and if you break them, you're in trouble.

The sun was level with his eyes, and his goggles didn't help much. From minute to minute they were spattered from old puddles.

The big green signs for the interstate appeared. Entrance ramps two miles ahead. Five bikers passed going the other way. Not the Duke. Now the entrance was a mile ahead. Still no solitary rider. I-93 NORTH NEXT RIGHT, SOUTH SECOND RIGHT. Then there was a profusion of directions: 3 going one way, 3A another.

Only a pickup was on the north ramp, and the northbound lanes were empty of bikers. Nat took the great bridge across the interstate, scanning the southbound side. A tractor trailer, a handful of cars — he slowed — not a single bike.

Then he saw him. The Duke came around the curve of the southbound entrance ramp. Nat knew instantly that it was the Duke. Even in the failing light, he recognized the upright posture of the Harley rider, the size and ease that marked the Duke, the faintest gleam of purple fenders.

Nat leaned into the sharply banked-down turning curve, accelerating as he came out, straightening up. A second later he rode beside the Duke.

The Duke raised his hand, shifting down, slowing. "Hey, man, I took you for smart. That's no place back there."

"Cy's in jail," Nat shouted.

"He's where?"

The Duke waved toward the shoulder and pulled off. He eased the helmet from his bandaged head and pressed his forehead a moment.

"That scene's a bummer. Where's Cyrus?"

"He's in jail. The cops think he threw the bottle."

"That's ridiculous. We were together."

"They won't believe it. I tried to tell them. They've booked him on assault with a deadly weapon, disorderly conduct, and resisting arrest. And they've got a hanging judge, too, who hates dirty bikies. You're the only one who can tell them he didn't do it."

The Duke muttered something.

"Will you turn back?"

The Duke looked down the broad interstate. The late summer evening darkened the distance. He looked at Nat, at Gage. He exhaled and eased his helmet onto his throbbing head. Then he twisted the throttle, bumped across the median, across the northbound lanes, and onto the exit ramp toward Laconia.

30

Finals

*In a spirit of peace, joy and fellowship we
proclaim to the nation that bikers are beautiful!*

— La Salette priest

The crowd outside the police station was smaller now. A cruiser pulled under the covered entrance, and two drunk bikers were hustled inside to be booked. A few riders stood at the desk, arguing or trying to think of arguments, when Nat and Gage came in with the Duke. He strode to the counter and leaned over it. The seated desk sergeant looked up quickly.

"I understand you've booked Cyrus Coombs for hitting me with a bottle."

"He hit somebody — allegedly."

"I want you to drop the charges. I don't know who did it, but I know he didn't." The Duke's voice was deep and full and persuasive. Nat smiled with relief. "Cyrus is a friend of mine — has been for six years."

"Ninety-three percent of all murders are committed by people who know each other."

"That has nothing to do with me and Cyrus." The Duke

leaned farther over the desk. "You can't hold a man without charge."

"These are pretty serious charges — assault with a deadly weapon, disorderly conduct, resisting an officer — I don't have the authority to just erase 'em."

"I'm the one that got hit, man! And I'm telling you, he didn't do it. I'm not charging him so you don't have a case."

"Can't do it tonight, sir. Once he's booked he's booked. You can tell it to the judge tomorrow morning. We're holding a special session of the court. We've got quite a few cases, you know — about three hundred, I'd say, and it's still Saturday night."

"But he's telling you! Cyrus didn't do it!" Nat yelled, and Gage was yelling, "You look pretty pleased booking three hundred — you're going to make a mint in fines, aren't you?"

The sergeant glared at them, and the Duke gripped Nat's arm and Gage's arm, one in each hand, and steered them out the double doors.

"Never insult the law. Argue but no insults, you hear?"

"What can we do?" Nat asked.

"You go back to the camp. I'm going to the motel. I'll meet you here at nine A.M. tomorrow." He turned to his machine, muttering, "Three hundred! There'll never be another National in this place." He hit the electric start and rode away.

Fatigue surged through Nat, and he fumbled getting his bike going. Now Gage leaned against his back like an exhausted child. They stopped by the Home of the Whopper and had hamburgers and Cokes, which gave them something to get back to camp on. Nat felt reasonably sure Cy would get off free. Gunning it up the last rise to their camp, he trembled with relief.

Gage swung off and took off her helmet and loosened her damp hair from its braid. Nat rolled his bike back on the center stand and stood up. For a moment they looked at each other. Gage said, "I wonder what those baton twirlers got arrested for — indecent exposure, disorderly conduct or immoral acts."

An instant Nat looked at her. He'd forgotten them. Then he saw them again in his head, and he burst out laughing. Gage laughed. They laughed until their stomachs hurt and the tears came and they staggered about bumping into each other, trying to draw breath. When they managed to stop, they were looking at each other again.

"I'm sorry about your jacket," Nat said. He brushed the back of his hand over the hardened bloodstain.

"It's all right." She smiled at him.

"It's kind of wet to sleep outside."

She nodded. "I think I'll come inside with you."

Rain pelted on the tent roof most of the night.

It was after nine the next morning when Nat and Gage arrived at the depot police station. Dozens of bikes were parked outside, and the police who stood about seemed less hostile than the night before.

"Lucky it rained," one officer said, and Nat mumbled, "I thought of that."

Bikers and their girls went in and out the doors leading to the old waiting room converted to municipal court.

Nat and Gage had just left the BM when Cyrus and the Duke came out the double doors. Cy looked dark and angry, and he swore, "Goddam — disorderly conduct! Twenty-five bucks!" The Duke had him by the arm and made sure he kept moving away from the station. Then Cy saw Nat, and his face brightened. Nat laughed, and Cy put his arms around him and pounded his back and said, "The Duke told me, man, you are all right!" He squinted and grinned and kissed Gage. "You are, too — for a woman, that is."

"I'll let that go for now," Gage laughed. "Why'd they pick you up, anyway?"

"I took off after the guy who threw the bottle, and the cops saw me runnin', but they didn't see him. The first thing I knew one of them tapped me on the skull with his stick." He grinned, but his eyes narrowed. "It's just as well. I'd have killed that guy, if I'd caught him."

The Duke put his hand on Cy's shoulder for a moment. Then he scanned the clear sky and said, "Beautiful! They'll hold the finals today. No doubt about it."

They put away a huge brunch at the Captain's Table and rode out once more toward the track. The 106 traffic had grown heavy again, but the taunting lines of bikers hadn't reassembled. A few riders watched dully from the shade trees beside the road. Others packed up. Gear was spread out to dry, and trash lay like a carpet from the pavement into the woods. Beer cans, pop cans, Styrofoam cups, furry paper plates, Colonel Sanders buckets and boxes were strewn sodden and molding everywhere.

"Tomorrow this state is going to wake up," the Duke said, "and realize what happened to it. It's going to mean trouble for bikers."

"Some of them deserve it," Gage said.

"Some," the Duke said.

Through the afternoon they sat packed into the stands with thousands of others while the production machines, the 125s, the 250s, roared and shrieked lap after lap over the great looping track. In one race Gary Scott rode a Harley-Davidson 250 to win, which pleased the Duke and Cyrus immensely.

"About time, man," Cy said, and the Duke agreed. "Make those Japanese move over."

Just before one start, a bike and rider shot out of control and plopped into the pond beside the front-straight. There was some laughter in the stands, but not much. A hot bike can do funny things, and most of the watchers knew it.

Nat watched the racers leap forward from the start, the gang-up loosening, stretching out by the first curve. Glancing down the row, he saw Cy stand up, popping a beer can but not thinking about it, watching intently, saying something to the Duke, who nodded. This was Cy's world. He fit into it, he had a place in it, and he was good at it. And Nat thought of himself. I've done all right, he thought. I get along in this world, but I'm not into it the way Cy is.

"What are you thinking about?" Gage shouted in his ear, and he grinned, "Me and bikes and the road — and — me mostly."

"Everybody's got to sooner or later." She smiled. "There's more than one road, Nat."

He saw her lips form the words more than he heard them. They were lost in the shouts and screams and shrieking machines as the bikes, strung out now, flew down the straight into the second lap.

In the great race of the day the lead changed sixteen times, the stands screaming and shouting encouragement that no racer could possibly hear. The lead shifted from Gary Nixon to Kenny Roberts to Nixon to Gene Romero and back to Nixon. In the end Nixon brought his electric green Suzuki first across the finish line. After the other contestants exited for the paddock, he made another lap. Alone this time, he took the black and white checkered flag from the official, thrust its stick into his left boot, and circled the course again. The banner fluttered in triumph while the crowd cheered.

The machine hadn't made Nixon, Nat thought, watching and yelling with the rest of them. The bike didn't make the man, and the man didn't make the machine, either. They both had to have class.

After the races Nat, Cy, Gage and the Duke tried to say things to each other as they stood around their bikes, but it was hopeless. The starting and throttling of a thousand machines, the crush to get out and away made it impossible.

The Duke silently put his arms around Cy and hugged him. Then he kissed Gage and held Nat for a moment. He and Cyrus embraced each other again. Nat saw his full lips form the word, "Beautiful! Beautiful!" The Duke settled himself on his machine, hit the electric start, grinned at them as he checked it out and fastened his helmet. The next moment he entered the mainstream of bikes, and they watched him go.

When they could, the trio worked their way through the traffic south to the camp again. There Cy said, "I don't feel real friendly toward this state. How about hittin' the road tonight?"

"I'm ready to get out of here," Nat said. After a moment's thought he added, "What about you riding with me this trip — in the spirit of brotherhood?"

"That's what it's all about," Cy grinned.

Swiftly they struck the little orange tent and packed their gear on the back ends of the two bikes.

"Do you think you'll sell it?" Cy asked as they pulled the tension cords tight.

Nat shook his head. "No — I really like it, but I'm a guy who has a bike — you know what I mean?"

Cy straddled the seat, trying it for room. "Yeh, I know what you mean. You're a guy with a bike. I'm a biker." He and Nat looked into each other's eyes and grinned, and Cy turned to Gage. "And she's a woman with a bike."

"And this woman's biking time is running out, too. I have to go back to the books one of these days soon."

They looked at her.

"We may be comin' to the end of the road," Cy said.

"I'd rather think of it as a fork," Gage said. "There'll be another one to get into, I hope."

"There's always another road," Nat said. He stomped hard on the kick start and mounted his BMW. Cyrus settled behind him. Gage swung on her red Honda and hit the button. They smiled at each other. Then, side by side, they bumped downhill and moved into the stream of motorcycles flowing away over the blacktopped road.